PETS

Tyrant Books
c/o Giancarlo DiTrapano
Via Egiziaca a Pizzofalcone
Napoli 80132
Italia

www.nytyrant.com

ISBN 978-1-7335359-9-1

First Edition

Book design by Wah-Ming Chang and Adam Robinson
Cover design by James Dillenbeck

PETS

AN ANTHOLOGY

Edited by Jordan Castro

CONTENTS

Introduction

There is nothing I would like more than to let these twenty-one essays, poems and fictions speak for themselves. That way I would not have to write this. They do speak for themselves; in fact, I'd like to recommend that the reader turn now to the first page and begin.

But if you really want to keep reading this introduction, Hi. Thank you for picking up or buying this book.

On December 14, 2016, I tweeted, "i want to start a lit mag called 'pets' where ppl write about their pets." My own pet, a dog named Kevin, had become my muse; I couldn't seem to write anything that didn't prominently feature interacting with him—pulling up thick handfuls of his fur or patting him thuddingly; calling him "Bunty" or "Bunty chingrata" or other derivative combinations of "buddy." I read J. R. Ackerley's masterpiece *My Dog Tulip*; I wanted to read more about other people's pets. To my surprise, almost no literary projects specifically about pets existed.

In order to prepare for this introduction, I read about the history of pets; I read introductions to other anthologies; I read about the history of silent reading; I edited this anthology. I thought I could avoid a meta-introduction; I would craft something uncharacteristically masterful in which I connected historical fact to aspects of each piece, as well as my experience with Kevin.

Something I thought I might do was this: state the number of years we, as a species, have been domesticating other animals as pets; state the number of years we, as a species, have been reading silently to ourselves; then tell readers that before they read the rest of this anthology, they should get a pet, because they're more evolved to do that than read silently, and therefore a pet would fulfill them more deeply and likely enhance the reading experience. One of the first things I told people after I got Kevin was that reading was "so much better with a dog." If I could edit the readers' experience, I'd edit it as such.

It turns out, though, that there is exhaustive debate about the way our ancestors read (some say we only read aloud until relatively recently while others say we've read silently for much longer), as well as inconsistent findings with regard to how long we've domesticated animals as pets, what constitutes a "pet," et cetera. Frankly, much of academic writing about pets is unseemly, incomprehensible, and beside the point. The writing that follows is, if I can say so myself, anything but.

In this anthology, pets are catatonic, saviors, victims, psychopaths, car companions, nearly extinct, dead, fake, loved, and cost $10,000. They are the cause of peed pants, ritualistic kite flying, and revenge. They are the objects of "fixation" and longing and lust (just kidding), as well as mediums through which we can talk about family, culture, morality, language, history, emotions, and, as is the case with all writing, ourselves.

Sitting in my chair, staring blankly, I just thought, "Voice of the voiceless." *Assumes a grandiose, speech-like tone.* I am the voice of the voiceless, speaking for these essays, which themselves are the voices of the voiceless: pets cannot speak for themselves. I am the voice of the voice of the … okay, all right. I again encourage the reader to turn the page and start reading.

JORDAN CASTRO

2019

PETS

The Measure of Love

Michael W. Clune

Weak people ignorant of history and devoid of common sense sometimes imagine that love cannot be measured. They are wrong: everything has a measure. The measure of love is vengeance. The magnitude of your love is directly related to the severity of the revenge you are prepared to exact.

By this measure, dogs have truly earned the name of man's best friend. History is littered with the mangled corpses of those who have insulted or threatened or even appeared to threaten their human companions. Subjected to the same measure, the human love of dogs is not found wanting. In the ancient Icelandic *Saga of Burnt Njal*, the killing of the protagonist's dog Bill inspires him to a self-denying orgy of horrific violence remarkable even in annals of this warlike people. Peter the Great was known to put whole villages of peasants to the sword for an injury done to a favorite hunting dog, earning him the sobriquet some of us still use in the emperor's memory: Peter the Loving.

I am a dog lover in this noble tradition.

The object of my love is Laila. She is a rescue dog—she suffered from the parvo that killed her littermates and was nursed back to health by a vet working pro bono. We adopted her in May 2011, when she was three months old. The good vet named her Laila, after one of Muhammad Ali's daughters, who had apparently also survived a difficult childhood illness. During the first weeks with us, her left ear flopped over her tiny face, and she shivered with fright, peeing when touched. She cried at night, so I developed an evening ritual of patting and comforting until she fell asleep, only then creeping upstairs to my own bed.

As her fear receded, Laila's sweet good nature gradually emerged, along with her playful intelligence. Laila is about forty pounds, with a thick and indescribably soft two-tone coat, black on top and white beneath. In her large brown eyes the immaterial substance of consciousness is suspended in its purest form. Her breed remains somewhat mysterious. My mother once met a dog closely resembling Laila at a fair in Wisconsin. The owner said the dog was an Australian kelpie. I have examined images of kelpies on the internet and found some that really do look like Laila. I have also found examples of the breed with heads of a coarse shovel-like shape alien to my friend's nature. I remain uncertain about her breed, which has sharpened my sense of her individuality. I think of her as an example of the kind of dogperson she is: the best such example, and the only one.

Among the many nicknames we discovered for Laila, one came to predominate: Burt. I find the syllable deeply satisfying, an aural kernel of fondness capable of adornment by various prefixes:

Sweetburt, Sillyburt, Lazyburt, Underburt, etc. Once my wife, Lauren, had occasion to refer to Laila by her nickname in an email to me, spelling it Bert, which disturbed me. She explained that the comic strip *Dilbert* featured a dog named Dogbert, and she figured that was the origin of Laila's nickname. I explained that I've never read *Dilbert*. Laila's nickname is spelled Burt.

By June I had composed my first poem about Laila:

> If you don't love my little Burt
> I will shoot you until your body squirts.

When walking Laila, I added to the poem over several weeks, composing numerous stanzas, all with the same form. The first line describes Laila's sweet nature, and the second expresses a violent threat against anyone who doesn't appreciate her. These poems represent the spontaneous outflow of my feelings for my medium-sized dogfriend, who trotted beside me, stopping occasionally to sniff trees and plants.

I read somewhere that, for a dog, sniffing represents the same vivifying aesthetic function as looking does for humans, and so, as I admired the skies of June, I modified my pace to enable Laila to experience the summer scentworld. No communication between us of our different sensory experiences of the world is possible, except in the crudest sense, when one of us warns the other of a threat, for example. This incommunication caused me sorrow for a time. But eventually I came to understand that our experiences are complementary. When I walk through the world with Laila, the underside of my vision is a warm, dark, buzzing complex of scents—as when you lift a rake that has lain all summer on the lawn, and find it has become a home for beetles, spiders, and worms.

I look down on those who walk without dogs, protruding their poor bare shivering sight into the world alone. Images have a brittle, two-dimensional cast for such walkers, lacking the complement of a dog's nose, ungrounded in the rich invisible odorous side of nature.

BLACK SUNDAY, THE day on which my love for Laila was to be measured, occurred on the second weekend of August 2011. The event that gave the date its name occurred on a walk. Our walks took two forms. In the shorter form, a "Friendship Patrol," we proceeded about half a mile from our house to a little park, which we looped. In the longer form, the "Friendship Parade," we proceeded a half mile past the little park to a larger park surrounding the local middle school, which we looped.

On that Sunday afternoon, it was already quite warm, in the mid-eighties, and I wondered whether it wouldn't be best, considering the heat, to go for a Friendship Patrol. But it had rained all the previous day, and Laila seemed fresh and eager for exercise once we'd reached the small park, so we decided to keep going.

To understand the events that follow, you must remember that Laila—while by now very attached and affectionate to me, and to family members, and indeed to anyone who got to know her and treated her with kindness—remained shy of strangers. Compared with the facile eager sociability of some dogs, her shyness might appear somewhat pathological. My own view is that, if there is pathology, it lies with those other dogs, and with a society that weans dogs from their natural protective and jealous love of their companions to approximate the inane smiling *good nature* of suburban neighbors.

This kind of friendly good nature is a phenomenon we have grown so accustomed to that we can no longer see it. To cleanse our eyes, we must return to the nineteenth century, to the acute minds who examined the qualities of our world when they were still new. Nikolai Gogol, in the immortal *Dead Souls*, gives us an insightful portrait of friendly *good nature* with the character Manilov. Gogol writes that the moment you meet Manilov, you think, *What a delightful person!*

The second moment you think nothing.

And the third moment you think, *What the devil kind of a man is this?*

Laila lacks friendly good nature in this diseased modern sense. She is loving rather than friendly, deep rather than superficial. On that summer Sunday, as we left the first, smaller park, I watched with a sinking heart as a smiley-faced stranger approached with a dog. This animal presented a cartoon version of its owner's demented good cheer, straining at the leash to bestow its unearned kisses on Laila's tender flank.

"Is your dog friendly?" the neighbor asked, in the same tone and with the same expectation with which he (or she; I didn't examine it closely) might ask: "Isn't it a beautiful day?"

"No," I said.

It was nothing but the simple truth, an honest answer to the neighbor's question, and a necessary one, to avoid unpleasantness. The neighbor's face fell, and for several seconds Laila and I received a glimpse of the inhuman coldness that lurks behind the desperately smiling face of social good nature. The individual and its dog stomped off.

"If you don't love my little Burt ..." I whispered to myself as we walked on.

———

AS VIOLENCE IS shortly to erupt into this true story, I must pause to remove a possible misconception. Laila is not friendly, but neither is she vicious. If I had allowed the stranger to approach with its dog, Laila would not have bitten either of them. She would simply have become upset, straining to get away, crying and barking. It was to prevent this undignified scene that I insisted the neighbor keep its distance. Laila would never bite without good reason. The core of her nature is a compassion that flies from harming any living thing, just as it shrinks from the advances of aggressive degraded false friendliness. A brief anecdote will illustrate Laila's compassionate nature.

When Lauren moved in with us, she brought her cat, Rasputin. Laila is doglike in her distaste for cats, but we introduced them slowly, as per the instructions on the SPCA website, and they became close friends, frequently curling up together on the couch. (It is true that occasionally Laila will become slightly jealous of any excessive attention shown to Raz.)

Raz—while in many respects charming and even doglike himself in his affection for his human friends—suffers from the common defect of his species in being a coldhearted sadistic killer who delights in meaningless torture. One day, Lauren saw a mouse that Raz had murdered lying on the living room floor. Laila came up to the mouse, and after sniffing it, began licking it tenderly and nudging it with her nose. Lauren believes that Laila was attempting to comfort or heal the poor mouse. An incident from my own experience supports this interpretation. Once, when I slipped and fell on ice, Laila ran up to me and began licking my face in the same loving, concerned, and compassionate manner observed by Lauren with respect to the mouse.

The absence of what the world calls friendliness in Laila is supplied by the presence of genuine compassion, and the capacity for real love.

Equipped with a better sense of Laila's nature, we will now return to the walk that was to give Black (or Bloody) Sunday its name. The glancing blow we had suffered from the friendliness of the neighbor near the small park was but a prelude to the blood-soaked torrent of friendliness we were shortly to encounter at the big park.

LOMOND MIDDLE SCHOOL, which dominates the big park, is a large brick Georgian structure constructed in the early twentieth century, soon after the founding of Shaker Heights. Walking down Lomond Avenue, Laila and I passed by the building, then turned right, where the sidewalk proceeds down a hill, orbiting the playground, ball park, and large open field behind the school.

At the very bottom of the hill, looking up, one sees in the summer a rising expanse of green grass, with the upper stories of the school peeking over the hill at the far end. This sight never fails to remind me of the images of green grass and blue sky associated with advertising campaigns for the Windows operating system (to which I have always been loyal, and which underlies the word processor in which I am typing these words). The default desktop background of Windows 95, which was rolled out when I was in high school, featured a gently rising hill of green grass crowned by a vibrant blue sky. The image on a desktop background quickly becomes associated with a feeling of excitement, of imminence, of prelude. It is a space of possibility—a space in which *something is about to appear*.

On that Sunday, when Laila and I reached the bottom of the sidewalk's park-circling loop, we paused as we usually did. Laila sniffed the air. I looked at the beautiful rise of grass, wondering again at its mysterious atmosphere of imminence.

I drew a deep breath.

Laila's nose twitched.

Four heads appeared over the hill's crest, followed by four bodies. They swiftly enlarged as they moved down the hill toward us. They were running. Two large dogs, leashless, as I saw to my horror, followed by two male or female humans. (I didn't examine them closely enough to discern which.) Now the dogs were close enough that I could see the red tongues hanging from their mouths. The oversized people laughed as they bounced down the hill. One of them was yelling rhetorically:

"IS YOUR DOG FRIENDLY?"

Laila backed up, whining. In the split second before the dogs hit us, I tried to shield her with my body. Then they were upon us, snuffling and pawing at her, while she twisted in her leash, frantically trying to get away. I grabbed one of the dogs by its collar and pulled it away from her—but the other dog, in a manic frenzy of friendliness, began to *lick her face*. In a series of desperate contortions, Laila slipped free of her collar and ran away up the hill. She was lost to sight in seconds.

I STOOD HOLDING her empty leash as the people at last reached me.

"Where'd your dog go?" said one.

"Come here, Rosco," said the other. "There's a good boy."

I ran up the hill looking for her. I scanned the lawns, the trees and porches where she might have taken shelter. Nothing. A car rumbled down Lomond. *Not in the street,* I prayed. *Please don't let her be in the street with these cars coming!*

But the street was empty. Where could she be?

"Laila! Laila dog!"

I called her name in the stifling August noon, jogging up and down the blocks, sweat blinding me. Finally, I spotted two young boys sitting on a porch across from the school.

"Have you seen a lost dog?" I asked. "A puppy, black fur with white markings?"

One of them just pointed at me. With nightmare clarity I thought, *He's pointing at me. I have become my own dog; I have been turned into my own dog!*

In a fraction of a second the madness had passed—the kid was pointing behind, not at me. I spun around, and there, on the doorstep of the school's massive front portal—which must, to her frightened senses, have resembled some Ur-version of the door of our own Georgian-style house—lay my little friend. She was panting desperately when I reached her, hyperventilating. She had broken off one of her nails in her flight, and blood matted her fur, blood that soon covered my T-shirt. I no longer trusted the collar, so I picked her up in my arms and began to walk her home.

After a quarter mile her panting grew worse—she was dehydrating; the temperature was now easily in the mid-nineties—and she lay heavy in my arms, but I couldn't move any faster. My own body heat probably exacerbated her distress.

Luckily I had my phone on me, so I called home. Laila and I waited in the shade of a nearby tree until my wife's car arrived.

"Did you see who did this to her?" she asked.

"Yes," I said.

Once we got home, we put Laila on the cool wooden floor and held the water dish to her lips. She lapped faintly. We applied blood-clotting ointment. I stroked her burning head.

"You're safe now," I whispered.

MY FRIEND DAVE once made an observation about gun ownership. Everyone knows, he said, that your chances of getting shot increase when you own a gun. The reasons for this aren't hard to understand—the risks of accident, of losing a gun battle with an intruder, suicide, etc. Dave estimated that your chances of getting shot increase by up to 80 percent when you own a gun.

But, he said, when you don't own a gun, your chances of shooting the person who violates you go all the way down to zero.

Mathematically, gun ownership wins by 20 percent. But I foolishly had sold my last gun several years before, when I lived in Florida. I remember the moment clearly. I'd gotten back from doing some volunteer work at a local facility for juveniles and had about fifteen minutes before I had to leave to go the Zen Center for the nightly meditation session. Just enough time to clean my gun. I had a new clip for my Glock and decided first I'd load that up.

I was pushing the 9 mm rounds into the clip, cursing as the shells bruised my thumb, wishing I'd bought one of the new extender clips so I'd have to reload less frequently. I examined the deep bruise on my right thumb. I imagined one of my friends at the Zen Center asking me how I'd gotten it.

Maybe this gun stuff, I thought, *doesn't really go with my new positive lifestyle.*

The next day I sold it. And three years later, as I sat next to my bleeding dehydrated Laila on Black Sunday, I regretted my decision, just as Dave promised I would.

"Dig a pit," said my wife. "In their front yard. Fill it with sharpened stakes, throw a length of AstroTurf across it."

"The mailman," I said.

"Fuck the mailman."

"Stake pit," I mused. "I like the primitive quality of the concept. The stakes, representing a dog's teeth or claws ..."

I considered. AstroTurf wouldn't work. For it to be convincing, the pit would have to be covered with some kind of net, with a thin layer of real sod spread on top. I doubted my competence to create such a device, let alone to transport and install it. Plus the idea of digging a pit, even at night, in this heat ...

"I've got a better idea."

THE IDEA OF "excessive" punishment highlights the classic problem faced by everyone who plots an act of revenge. How do you match the vengeance to the crime? How—to quote the great source on the topic—do you apply the "eye for an eye" principle when the offense involves something less easily delimited than a single organ?

A literal interpretation of the "eye for an eye" equation is unsatisfactory for several reasons. With such an interpretation, my revenge on the Laila-violators would be best served by rushing at them in such a way as to cause them to flee. What this ignores is the vast discrepancy between Laila's experience of the world and the calloused, habit-worn sluggish dull sensations of the irresponsible dog-owners I pursued. Laila's experience of flight on Black Sunday is in no way equivalent to what the owners would feel were I to jump out from behind a bush in a gorilla suit, for example, making terrifying noises and waving my arms. They'd freeze; then, if I was lucky, maybe run a few feet. But when they saw I wasn't pursuing, they'd stop, take a better look at me, and either yell at me angrily or, more likely, laugh.

But what was Laila's experience during her flight? Boundless, bottomless terror. Lacking a framework with which to understand the limits of her danger, she must have felt that her world had collapsed. Her friend stood powerless as terrible ravening beasts rushed at her, intent no doubt on her utter destruction. So she fled, heedless of where she ran, believing in no safe haven, running in utter devouring terror, tearing her claw in the frantic scramble to—where? She had nowhere to go. Nowhere was safe. When she could run no more she simply collapsed in a doorway that offered some distant resemblance to her lost home—but which she knew could offer none of home's protection.

So how, I asked myself, could I match Laila's subjective, interior experience, to a necessarily external, objective act of vengeance on her assaulters? I reflected. What better way than to brand a letter on their flesh? A letter—fundamental symbol of Language—and what was language but a door, swinging between inside and outside, subjectivity and objectivity, self and other? I would brand their cheeks with a letter—the mark of the passage between the dark privacy of experience and the sunlit world of matter—a passage denied by nature to my little friend!

Finding a branding device in a modern suburban home is not easy. We needed an iron or a metal "L," attached by a stick, which we could heat and then apply to the perpetrators' faces. We didn't have anything like this in the house. The closest thing we found was two butter knives, but the "L" would have been far too large, and there was no easy way to handle the heated knives in any case.

Then my eyes lit upon the stovetop—the iron circles of the burners—and I had an inspiration. Laila's last name, of course, was the same as my own: Clune. By pressing the offender's face down on half of the burner, it would create a "C," or, even better, a series of "C"s: CCC.

NO LINE DIVIDES the love that binds you to a victimized friend or family member from the actual process of vengeance. The idea of such a boundary has been unfortunately popularized by works of literature: when Odysseus slays the suitors, for example, or the Count of Monte Cristo tracks down and serves sentence on his betrayers, the author focuses on the bloody details, the mechanism of revenge; love is nowhere to be found. The author portrays the love Odysseus feels for Penelope before and after he murders the suitors—not during.

Yet here I believe the authors are simply taking a narrative shortcut, distributing in time for the purposes of the story what is in life concentrated in a single fused reality. My own experience, at any rate, is that the very process of revenge brings us closer to the loved one. In finding and punishing Laila's violators, I also learned and discovered wonderful new features of my little friend.

But there are others, better suited to deliver the details of my vengeance and my love with the vivacity they deserve. If, while visiting the quiet suburb of Shaker Heights, Ohio, you happen to meet a couple with three "C"s burned onto their faces—the largest ones completely obliterating their right eyes—ask them. Don't be shy.

Ask them exactly how much I love Laila.

FRANNY

Patty Yumi Cottrell

In mid-July I wrote a document about my cat. I began this document with a memory of my cat, when she was a kitten. In the memory, it is the summer of 2005; my cat was lying on my stomach as I sat in an IKEA chair watching Todd Solondz's *Storytelling*. I was twenty-four years old.

I had never had my own pet before. And I didn't even want this cat; some well-meaning loveable stoner-type coworkers thrust her upon me. Elisa and Johanna brought this cat into the café where we worked tirelessly and said mean things to customers. "Patty, this is for you." I didn't like cats. I thought they were evil. I wanted a dog, not a cat. I took her home anyway. My cat was a tiny black ball that fit into my hand. She was vocal. I left work early that day, and when I got home, I searched my bookshelves for a name. I saw a book with two names in the title. I chose one of those.

A few days after she came home with me, she fell into the toilet. She was clumsy, and she simply fell into the bowl after I had urinated. I wasn't good at flushing then. I had to go to work so I didn't do anything. I thought perhaps the urine would "dry off" her fur and "go away." When I came home, the apartment had the foulest smell imaginable, worse than any cage at the zoo.

It's August and I cannot find the document I began in mid-July. I have looked at the folder on my desktop titled "[my cat's name]," but the document is not there. Instead there are various medical records and examinations and blood tests and results from an ultrasound and a meeting with a feline internist, and a diary of my cat's stools, what type of stool she had, whether it was soft or hard, and how many, and when.

My cat has not been feeling well. I have talked about my cat with many strangers and friends. One friend told me she couldn't imagine how I was coping with my cat's health issues because I have anxiety and depression. She has pancreatitis and kidney disease. She might have IBD, small cell lymphoma, diabetes, hyperthyroidism, etc. Whatever it is, I want to know. My therapist, a Buddhist-ordained priest, said that one of the themes of my life is searching for the truth.

When my brother committed suicide, I wanted to know everything about it. I scoured his closet for clues, and there were medical records detailing his attempt to donate his organs. I reached out to a friend of his from grade school. I eavesdropped on people's conversations at the funeral. I wrote a book about that. When I finished it, I felt better. Then, for a year or so I was very broke. My cat became sick in January of 2018. I had to borrow a hundred dollars from a friend so I could take her to the vet. My parents suggested I give her up for adoption since I couldn't afford to take care of her.

"You can't afford to own a goldfish," said my father. My cat was thirteen years old and black. If she went to the Humane Society she would spend the rest of her life in a cage. "No," I said firmly. I have a shaved head. I am skinny and Asian. I imagined putting on a wig and going on SeekingArrangement. I would do whatever it took. "Absolutely not," I said to him.

She had an eye infection. Then she had feline chin acne. There were spells of not eating or drinking water. This went on for some time. In March, I won two literary awards, ostensibly to be used for writing a new book. It was a miracle. When an awards committee told me about the prize over the phone, I started crying. Everyone cries when money comes out of nowhere. I would write three books with the money over the next two years. That's what I envisioned. Instead, as soon as I cashed the checks, I began to take my cat to different vets, to try to gather opinions about what was wrong. "Her symptoms are vague," said one vet. "It could be something sinister like cancer." Another vet told me to calm down, and assured me my cat was depressed because she didn't have access to an entire house, just a room in an apartment. My girlfriend was worried about me. She said I was "fixated."

My cat used to lie in the crook of my arm on the bed. She would lie on my stomach or between my legs. I wanted her to greet me when I opened the door. Perhaps this was selfish. I would go on to spend a significant amount of the prize money trying to find out what was wrong. Perhaps this was foolish and limited. But I had been foolish before. I had canceled events to stay home with my cat. I refused to travel anywhere. When I left my cat with my girlfriend for a few nights, because I absolutely had to, I was panicked. All I could think about was my cat. Did my girlfriend make sure to close the bedroom door so my roommate's cat wouldn't attack her? Did she fill the mason jar with water all the way up to the top, so that the water was practically brimming over? She sent me a photo of my cat and I zoomed in to look at the jar. "You didn't fill the jar all the way to the top," I texted her.

"It's spilling over," she said. "The photo is an optical illusion."

*

One night in April, sitting on the bed, my cat looked at my girlfriend and me and growled at us. She had never growled or hissed at me in her life. Even when I had to syringe Miralax into the side of her mouth. Even when I had to clip her nails. The growls seemed to emanate from her abdomen. Her eyes looked vacant and dull; I thought she might be dying. We took her to the ER. Seven hundred dollars later, we had no answers.

I read books about death and Zen Buddhism. I read books by Pema Chödrön, Charlotte Joko Beck, Shunryu Suzuki, and Joan Halifax. I began to write a new novel then stopped. I was caught in an obsessive loop. I went to The Strand and asked the bookseller where the books about death were located. He showed me a small section on a shelf in the basement. All of the books were about humans dying. I didn't care about that. I wanted to know what to do when your cat is dying. I should have been more specific. I glanced over the books about human death. I felt nothing. I felt like I was failing her. I resolved to do more.

I joined a feline kidney disease message group online. My cat was diagnosed with kidney disease two years ago. Maybe she was in renal failure. I posted my first post, a long wall of text about everything that was happening. Someone on the message board chastised me for taking too long to get the pancreatitis diagnosis. She said that my cat was in pain. The subtext was that I had failed my own cat. I spent an hour composing a response, detailing each vet visit—what I said, what the vet said, and how much money I spent. Now when I post a message on the board, only one or two people respond to me. The kidney disease message board people have shunned me.

I would be at a friend's house for dinner and somehow find a way bring up the topic of my cat. I would say things like, "She came into my life thirteen years ago ..." then start sobbing and leave the room.

My therapist says I am grieving the loss of the cat I once knew. I wish I could enjoy each day with my cat, but I wake up in the morning in a state of anxiety. I go into the bathroom and immediately gather all of her medications. I push pills down her throat. I read on the message board that these medications are bitter and foul-tasting so I cut them into tiny fragments with a knife, then put the fragments, practically a powder, into the tiny gel caps so my cat won't foam at the mouth or vomit. I syringe water into the side of her mouth. I stick a needle into her and give her fluids. Then I press a cotton ball into her fur to keep the fluids from leaking. A few hours later, I give her another pill.

This doesn't seem to be working.

My cat now sleeps in the litter box. This can mean a cat has a UTI. It can also mean a cat is dying. This morning I took my cat to the vet because of her "litter box behavior." The vet performed a physical examination. She said that my cat is obese and pre-diabetic. She said that it's possible my cat is hyperthyroid, because hyperthyroidism causes cats to "act weird." I asked her what was wrong with my cat. She said my cat has two diseases as it is, kidney disease and pancreatitis, and that they are incredibly frustrating for vets to treat. I told her I had scheduled an ultrasound, the second in the past four months, in a week and a half. She said that's fine.

"But if you really want to know what's going on, you might want to consider an exploratory surgery," she said.

I was staring at my cat who was resting on the table, looking at the wall with what I believed to be a certain amount of scorn.

"I go in there, and open up the length of her abdomen. Then I take out samples of each organ and send them off to a lab."

Propelled by curiosity, I asked how much it costs.

She paused. "It's very expensive."

I pictured my cat on a cold steel table with her abdomen open. I don't know what to do, I thought. Is this the right thing? My cat means more to me than my own family. My cat is "my obsession." But this is serious. If I did this, my girlfriend and parents would think I was crazy. I don't think I would have anyone's sympathy if she came home and stopped eating. Or if she died on the operating table. But part of me, the "fixated part," wants to know if there's cancer. If there's something malignant and growing, possessing her, eating her organs, etc. I want to know if she should be euthanized. Is this a solution? At what kind of cost?

"When you say expensive, do you mean like a thousand dollars?"

"It might be a lot more than that," said the vet.

We looked at my cat.

"But if you want to go all the way, if you really want to know what's wrong with your cat, then that's what I'd recommend."

Our appointment ended. I paid the medical bill with a credit card I reserved solely for my cat's medical needs. I put my cat into her carrier and took her out to the car. I drove for ten minutes, then I stopped at a gas station for cigarettes. I left the windows of my car cracked so my cat wouldn't suffocate. I looked up exploratory surgery on my phone as I stood in line. Someone on a message board said after the surgery her cat stopped eating and died. Someone else said it saved his cat's life. I put my phone away. A middle-aged man riding a child's bicycle in the parking lot asked me for five dollars or a cigarette. I gave him a cigarette.

It took thirty minutes to drive my cat home. As soon as I let her out of her carrier, she ran off to her favorite corner of the house. She wedged her fat body in between two bookshelves. She closed her eyes. I stroked her head then I gave her a medication and syringed Miralax and water into the side of her mouth. She growled.

As I type this document, my cat is still alive. She has ailments. She needs a lot of medication. She scratched her cornea. I squeeze an ointment into her eye throughout the day. Last weekend she smelled like urine. She sleeps for hours at a time, wakes up to eat and go to the bathroom, then falls asleep. In this part of my life, we have been each other's witness. She has seen me with various partners in numerous cities. She has seen me weeping on the floor. I have seen her burst out of a cardboard box, panting with happiness. I've seen her fall asleep on a pillow with her littermate. All of that is in the past; I expect very little from her now.

Dudu (2007–)

Tao Lin

My parents seemed on the verge of sustained, unconcealed bicker-ing. "Five more minutes," said my dad. Five minutes later, he still hadn't finished working, and seemed irritated. "One more thing," he said, and he began to quietly lecture my mom, muttering that all she did was bother him. My mom retreated to her office, where she depressedly said that, because it was getting late, we'd go someplace nearer, instead of Chiang-Kai Shek Memorial Hall, as we'd planned.

I asked my dad when he'd be ready, told my mom ("five more minutes"), got on the inversion table, started recording a Voice Memo, and began talking about how, as I became more limber and less inflamed, I could crack more of my bones, including, while inverted, ones in my sacrum. My dad finished working, stood, and asked if Dudu, our four-pound white toy poodle, was capable of using the inversion table. As we waited for the elevator, Dudu did yoga-like stretches, and I said, "She doesn't need it."

Outside, I began to fully realize that my parents had been bickering for at least a day. I decided to distract them with questions. I asked my mom what she'd thought, in July, when she'd weighed only ninety-five pounds—a question I'd planned to ask for weeks.

"I thought I had 'cancer.'¹ 'Cancer' causes sudden weight drop."

"Were you very scared?"

"Very worried. Not scared. If I had 'cancer,' it would be very inconvenient, needing to do this, do that."

"Did you tell Dad?"

"No. Telling him would be of no use."

Dudu chased my dad—her favorite person—as he ran ahead, saying, "Run, run, run, run." Each morning, she sat inside or outside the open-doored bathroom, guarding my dad as he sat on the toilet with two smartphones—emailing, messaging, checking the stock market, watching videos, listening to music.

"He doesn't know what's going on with me," said my mom.

"He knows," I said accusingly. "One day when you weren't home, Dad told me to check the 'internet' for what it meant that you lost two pounds suddenly."

My mom was quiet for five seconds.

"He does know what's going on with you," I said.

"I only tell Auntie," said my mom about her sister. "And Thin Uncle and Alex," she said about her brother and her other son, who was six years older than I was.

"In the past, have you told Dad before?"

"I've said, Ahyo! I only weigh such-and-such now."

---

1. Words in single quotes in dialogue were spoken in English; the rest of the dialogue was in Mandarin.

"When your weight only went down a little, he knew. He told me to check the 'internet.' He'd looked very 'worried,' and it had only been 'two pounds.' It was before you lost even more weight."

"It could be that there's 'worry,' but he won't say it," relented my mom.

My dad was ahead of us in the crowded plaza, carrying Dudu, who'd gotten scared and stopped walking. Four or five performers were singing through microphones and speakers.

"Have you told Auntie why you lost weight?" I said.

"I said it could be, if not 'cancer,' a 'thyroid' problem."

We walked for a minute.

"When I was switching medications," said my mom, about changing from synthetic to natural thyroid. A decade ago, a doctor had—unhelpfully, it seemed to me—removed her thyroid gland.

"Yeah," I said.

"It could be that, switching," said my mom, seeming uncertain.

"It was that," I said, surprised because I'd assumed we'd both known that excessive thyroid had been the main and probably only cause. I explained hyperthyroidism's connection to weight loss. A commercial plane, on its way to an airport two miles away, fumed past, lumbering and low, muting the Sunday crowd, maybe 30 percent of whom were there for the farmer's market.

"The 'director' of '*Split*' directed '*The Sixth Sense*,'" I said. "Have you seen it?"

"Yeah," said my mom. "The child, who sees ... I must have seen it with you."

"Child who sees what?" said my dad.

My mom didn't respond. Earlier that day, we'd seen *Split*—a movie about a man with twenty-three personalities. I'd told my mom that when children and elders in society had mental problems, they were brought to hospitals, where they became fucked. "You two are lucky," I'd said. "You don't have to fear me putting you in a 'hospital.' Even if you were 'insane,' I wouldn't." My mom had said, "You care," and I'd said that those who brought relatives to hospitals cared too.

"'Ghosts,'" I said.

"Most of the movies I've seen, I've seen with Tao," said my mom. We'd seen many movies together in Florida when I was a tween and teenager, after my brother had left for college, when my dad had usually been away on business.

"Ahyo—you haven't seen any movies," my dad told Dudu, setting her down on the sidewalk. "Tao saw so many movies as a child, and he's forgotten them all," he said confidently and idly. "Children watching movies isn't much use. It's all forgotten."

"I haven't forgotten," I said quietly after two seconds.

As my mom told a story involving me and something about jumping, my dad interrupted her, loudly saying, "Hey, are they digging something here? Look. Are they building something here?" My parents seemed to be vying for my attention. I was more interested in my mom, who continued reminiscing: how we'd often gone to restaurants, just us two—Steak and Ale, Olive Garden, Yae Sushi. "Once we sat, you'd say, Do you believe there is a 'God'?"

"And what would you say?" I said, surprised.

"I would just say there was," said my mom.

"I don't remember asking that," I said.

"You often asked it. At that time, you believed there was."

"What was one reason I gave for there being a 'God'?"

"Reasons, I can't say," said my mom. "I don't remember."

A train passed on an elevated track parallel to the sidewalk, Dudu pooped, we continued walking, and I thought, not for the first time, that how my parents treated Dudu (with attentive patience, sustained curiosity, unconditional love, and as an animate medium through which to talk to oneself or others) was probably how they'd treated me, when I'd been small and doglike.

Two minutes later, we noticed Dudu was catatonic.

She was forty feet behind us, standing motionless.

"Du, come," shouted my mom, and she clapped thrice.

"She hasn't walked here before," I offered.

"She has," said my mom.

After fifteen seconds, Dudu sat. For the next hundred seconds, as my dad took a business call, and my mom and I discussed pet dogs who'd been attacked by wild dogs, four or five of which lived in each of the three parks near my parents' apartment, a calmly seated Dudu stared at us. "If we see wild dogs, we should pick up Du, to be safe," said my mom. "Du would be dead in an instant. Thin Uncle's Mianmian was bitten by a wild dog, breaking his 'rib.' Mianmian was hospitalized many days."

"Come, child," shouted my dad after his call.

"A moment ago, she walked a little," I said.

"Walked two steps," said my mom.

"Du come, Du come," said my dad.

"She hasn't used that technique before—just walking a little," I said.

"She's thinking, Do I want to or not?" said my mom. "Come. Come. Du! Du, come on!" she shouted, then clapped seventeen times as another train passed. "Haven't seen a dog like this before."

We walked away a little, making Dudu fifty feet away.

Besides two steps, she hadn't moved in four minutes.

"Come, come," shouted my dad.

"People walking by are noticing her," I said.

"Go pick her up," said my dad, then he hid behind a bush.

"When she can't see you, she'll panic," I predicted.

"Is she coming?" whispered my dad.

After a moment, Dudu stood, but didn't walk.

"She still isn't," I said, laughing a little. "She knows we've waited a *very* long time before." Sometimes she seemed to want to go home or in a different direction. Sometimes she seemed depressed or like she wanted to rest. After a while, we'd follow her elsewhere, walk behind her to force her ahead, or carry her.

My dad whistled for five seconds.

Dudu sat.

"Sits down!" said my mom.

"Sits down," said my dad.

"She knows we won't leave her," I said. "She 'trust' us a lot." Alone in the distance, she seemed like a surreally wild or recently abandoned toy poodle. Once, my mom had said that Dudu most feared being alone, without companions.

"Normally, when she can't find me, she panics," said my dad. "I'll come out of hiding, then." He got on the sidewalk. "Du, let's go, Du," he said, returning to hiding.

"This time, we've waited so long, we must not let her win," I said.

"Is she sitting?" said my dad. "If she's sitting, someone will take her."

Dudu ignored a group of people as they passed her on the sidewalk.

"They're pointing," said my mom. "Go get her. A wild dog might run out."

I jogged to Dudu, picked her up, jogged back.

"If you didn't go to her, she'd have no dignity," said my mom. "If we ignored her, she'd have no dignity. No dignity. And because you went to get her, she was like, Okay, you've come, so I will walk."

"This time she's very happy," I said. "She waited so long, out-waiting us."

"This way, she has more dignity," repeated my mom.

"Next time, we'll need to wait even longer," I said.

"Someone will steal her," said my dad.

"Next time, we'll need to wait *too* long," I said.

"Longer and longer each time," said my dad.

"If we wait too long, someone will steal you," my mom told Dudu. "Do you understand? I heard one of those people say, There is a dog … that no one wants."

"Her hair is cut so short, she'll be cold," said a passerby in her fifties. People, with or without dogs, commonly criticized Dudu's nakedness. In winter in Taipei, every small dog wore clothes, and some wore shoes.

"No, she's not scared of the cold," said my dad.

"How do you know?" said the woman.

After a moment, my dad said, "When she wears clothing, she refuses to walk."

"Is that so?" said the woman.

"Dogs: let them run a bit and they won't be cold," said my dad.

"It's because she's young. If she was old—"

"Young?" said my dad. "She's nine."

"Nine counts as young," said the woman.

We continued walking. As we approached a ramp, which bikers, ignoring the sign that said not to, sometimes used, my dad, singing, "Hug, hug," picked up Dudu.

"She asked how we knew Dudu wasn't cold," I said.

"How would you respond?" said my dad.

"We don't know," said my mom.

"I do know," I said. "Wild dogs didn't used to wear clothes."

"Ah," said my mom. "Dogs of the past."

"It's healthier that way," I said. "If Dudu is a little cold, she'll move. 'Wild dogs' in the past all had to 'experience winter.' They were cold every 'winter.' For the whole 'winter.' 'Every year.'"

"Pet dogs are protected too much," said my mom.

"I wanted to tell her all this," I said.

"Why didn't you hurry and say it?" said my dad.

"Because it's too much information," I said.

"She said, How do you know she's not cold? and I suddenly didn't know what to say," said my dad, who'd recently begun preemptively telling passersby that Dudu was a "mountainclimbing dog"; from 2007, when she was born, to 2016, she'd mountainclimbed only once or twice, but it was only February 4, 2017, and she'd already mountainclimbed six times that year.

My mom brought up *Zhuangzi*, a book published 2,300 years earlier that had a story about how Zhuangzi saw minnows in a stream and said they were happy. Zhuangzi's companion responded, "You aren't a fish; how do you know they're happy?"

"Then what?" said my dad, who'd told me the story many times. "Fish are happy, then what? Tao, let Tao say it. What did the other person say? In response."

"I'm thinking," I said agitatedly, then gentler and carefully:

"He said the fish were happy, and the other person said, How do you know they're happy; you aren't them, and he said, You aren't me; how do you know that I don't know they're happy?"

"Ehh. Right, right!" said my dad excitedly. "This is 'logic.' And then what? If you add more?"

"If you aren't me, how do you know I don't know the fish are very happy," said my mom to herself.

"And then what?" said my dad aggressively. "You're not me, so you don't know. Then what? If you go one thought further. How do you do it?"

"Then it's endless!" said my mom.

"Then—no, no!" said my dad loudly. "Then—you say, You aren't me. How do you know that I don't know that you don't know the fish are very happy," he said, seeming to mangle it a bit, and laughed.

My mom laughed a little. "This is a little like—"

"I'm trying to think of a better 'answer,'" I said. "What you said, everyone knows."

"Just keep adding," said my dad.

I tried to think of a way to avoid the endless loop.

"Because I've been a fish," said my dad, and, looking at me, he made a self-conscious noise, seeming suddenly and briefly vulnerable.

A minute later, after I'd stopped the Voice Memo at twenty-eight minutes and thirty-nine seconds, my dad began talking about fishing. "Why do you have to mix up everything with fishing?" said my mom, making me feel magically like I was in a Raymond Carver story about a bickering couple. Amused, I emailed myself what she'd said.

It began to lightly rain, so we turned homeward. I told my parents I'd recorded the walk. They weren't surprised. They knew I'd been recording us for my novel. "I've written about fighting," I said. "I want to 'balance' it with good things now."

"So, today was good?" said my mom.

"Yes. I've already 'recorded' more than enough fighting."

With a smile, my mom said that I meant bickering (*chǎo jià*—吵架), not physically fighting or brawling (*dǎ jià*—打架), as she'd told me many times over decades.

Two minutes later, my dad dropped Dudu while picking her up, and she yelped loudly, and my mom told me about Dudu's childhood trauma. When Dudu was one or two, my dad had lifted her carrying case without closing it. She'd fallen on her head and had vomited. My parents had feared she had a concussion.

"But the worst was," said my mom, and then she told of how, on their way to the U.S. in 2008, they'd left a five-month-old, caged Dudu outside a pet store for half an hour. They hadn't anticipated the store being closed in the morning. They'd called Auntie, who'd located Dudu by following her continuous screams.

THE GREAT BIRD SEARCH

Nicolette Polek

My mother remembers five separate deaths: tumor, disappearance, mauled by neighborhood animal, injury, and a fly-away. I remember four different colors; together we recall three names. We had these birds over six years—I think. Much of my childhood is foggy and uncertain. It's shrouded, or sometimes replaced, by stories I've told myself and others. I'm concerned about why I can't remember our birds clearly. How many did we have? I adored them; they were our bright things in a dark house.

A scene that I remember: My piano teacher sitting in a green chair, bald and patient. I'm sitting beside him on a piano bench, grinning because I have a secret. I pull out Bach. I pull out Duvernoy's *School of Mechanism*. My piano teacher asks me what else I have in my bag. When I laugh, I look like a beaver; three index cards could fit between my front teeth. I reach to the bottom and pull out a cardboard box. A weight shifts around as I open the flaps. I place Nippy, a bright blue parakeet, onto the piano. I'm excited for him to sing when I play my scales. Instead he poops quietly on the Steinway.

Nippy's wings were clipped when we got him. Perhaps I thought I could encourage him to fly—I was five—so I threw him up in the air and he smacked into the ceiling. He crumbled down onto the bed, then wobbled back to life. Nippy was so beautiful; I didn't know what to do with him. I stuffed him into my shirt, in drawers and shoes; I ran after him through the house and my father brushed him off surfaces. Nippy learned three words, then developed a tumor from stress and died in my hand. I thought life and death would always be like this—violent, morbid, pretty.

Once, my father dreamt he was in the neighbor's yard, trying to reason with Nippy to come home. He was in his sleep clothes and the snow was melting. My blue bird scuttled away from his reach. My father spoke insistently to him, telling him that it was getting late and that his food and toys were next door. My father retells this often.

After Nippy, I don't remember. I consult my parents' photographs. Most of them are out of focus. We had a bad camera; I overzealously positioned the lens too close to the small birds. The blurriness makes it difficult to distinguish whether the plumage is light yellow, white, or light blue, all of which signify distinct birds in my memory. After careful consideration, I think these photographs are three different birds.

a. This one is sitting on a banker lamp, reading the "news." I would tape various paper "books covers" on the lamp for the bird to "read," though it chewed on the paper instead. This bird looks mostly white.

b. This bird seems yellowish and haggard, almost insect-like.

c. This one is the same color as my shirt, which is a light blue. I vaguely remember this one "begging" at the table, which would involve it sitting on my mother's shoulder, then quickly descending down her arm to grab something off the plate.

A friend reminds me that outdoor birds used to get trapped in my family's basement. Usually they were starlings. I would hear them banging in the vents. Once, an injured one clunked around for so long that my father took a broom to it and flattened it into the cement. My kid friends thought we were so brutal. They rumored my family to be living in ruins, sucking on rocks and committing strange crimes.

Other kids wondered why I didn't eat Lunchables or watch television, or why I wasn't allowed to go to the mall or sleepovers. That my parents are from another country felt insufficient, so I tried different explanations: My parents used to be circus performers! My mother is a butterfly scientist! We just moved to this country! Someone follows us with a knife! We are fluent in Esperanto! I am a spy! My childhood memories are a mix of fraudulence and exaggerations, tall tales I told as a kind of protection, which can make my memory-detective work tricky. My mythology of myself gradually became who I presented by default. I gave myself over to stories, leaving behind the facts, like my birds.

According to old diary entries, my other parakeets were named Pecky and Penelope. With names, I can begin to picture them dimensionally, place them in time. Pecky was definitely the white parakeet and Penelope was light blue. Penelope liked mirrors and doorknobs. Pecky liked to be pet on the neck. She would puff up and cock her head to the three o'clock position. I'd wiggle my finger below the beak, "under the chin" for her, and she'd close one eye. Beneath the feathers she was shrunken and bony like someone very old. When we spritzed her with a spray bottle, she became slender like a lizard. The other, nameless, yellow one I still can't imagine. All I know is that it was our last bird.

Perhaps the key to remembering the yellow bird is finding its name. I look through a list online. Popular names include Coco, Baby, Largo, Dunly, and Stephen King. Popular unisex names are Whisper, Touche, and Megabyte. I scroll through various websites expecting something in me to light up like a metal detector. I message a childhood friend who used to ride her bike over. She confirms only what I already know.

I mention my search to my therapist and he tells me about the parrots of Telegraph Hill. How a woman had let go of her cherry-headed conures in the nineties and now they've taken over an area of San Francisco. I remember that I've seen those parrots before in real life. I visualize the vibrant parrots in a tree along the sidewalk; I feel a jolt of a feeling similar to loss. And through that memory, I remember something else. I remember how I had also seen my yellow parakeet high up in a tree, through the back door of my parents' house that my father left open, then never seeing it again.

After that, it feels as if I always knew. It's funny, trying to remember an epiphany. I can write down what led to it—what my therapist said and how it unlocked something in me. But there is also an atmosphere to it, like a fog that pulses to show a walking path, or the settling of sediment that reveals a missing locket at the bottom of a pond. There is something mystical and frothy about the non-epiphany part of an epiphany. I remember it, but not exactly.

When I was hurt, I changed my stories to show it. I was certain my father took a broom to the starling in the basement, but when I ask my mother, she doesn't remember it. Maybe it was another thing I made up. Or maybe it was true in another way. With language, my pain became malleable—I could control it and change it. It's a common child's game that isn't fun as an adult. It's the opposite of an epiphany: the veil evaporates and I already know what's there. I just wish it weren't.

Not long ago I started to tell the truth. Old habits fell away slowly and stubbornly. I said what was true even if it was dull or embarrassing. Sometimes I would look at something like a sidewalk or a leaf and feel immense gratitude. A big-bellied robin belting in the yard would fill me with awe.

Nippy, Pecky, Penelope, Henry. This last name falls into place at a random moment, as I look up from a chair. I remember all their songs clearly. You could hear them inside the house from the driveway. They would sing on my mother's shoulder while she cooked. They would sing while we ate, along with the classical music on the radio, when I did homework. They would tuck one foot into their feathers and sing a little lullaby to themselves. They would land on my head and sing with their entire bodies, like alarms, as I walked through the house. They would hide behind the books and sing. They would sing along to thunder. Sometimes, they would sing at night.

LITTLE VIOLENCES ON THE FARM

Christine Schutt

The girl heard him before she saw him, Rhymer, from school, her tormentor, and just as he saw her, she moved from under the scruffy copse and ran full out for Fulmer's barn. No other shelter was near enough, and home was hardly safe. She slipped through the loose barn doors and down the aisle to the reinforced door with the jail-bar top where the bull, called Armor, lived. She leaned over out of breath. Rhymer wouldn't look for her here, and if he did, she had Armor for protection—ha, ha—old joke. Armor butted the bars with his putty-colored snout and chuffed small plumes of breath wetly; the girl's breath came out whiter.

Rhymer, bawling threats not so far from the barn, yelled her name, *Haawwwg!* and it shamed her, the ugliness of it, but what could she do? She was no fighter. In school, out of school, he lunged out of nowhere: *I'd like to see you slide down a razor blade naked.*

From outside, but close, came Rhymer's shrill whistle, a visible sound, followed by a blank. Was Rhymer lying in ambush, or had he moved on?

Before Rhymer, there was Michael Speech, who left a piece of shit on the toilet seat for her to sit on. *Did you like my present?* And before him came her cousins, Teddy and Jack, and the man who said he was her father: so many tormentors, and she was only eight.

A terrible quiet followed before the bull did something loud enough, and she ran, ran out of the barn and alongside the bent stalks of cow corn, past the hairy pigs, their coarse skin scrotally dark. They grunted on their way to the muddy trough to snort up slops and make pigs of themselves. They looked slimed and shiny in the light, weirdly metallic.

She ran to the end of the farmer's field, up past the rise, past the empty farmhouse and down the slope to home, home where the light inside was a different color—more blood in it. But before she went in, she stood at the edge of the road buckled with frost heaves and felt large trucks shake past. Where were they coming from, and where were they going so swiftly, escaping the little violences on the farm?

THE PARROT: NOTES ON THE GREAT EARTHQUAKE[1]

Ryūnosuke Akutagawa

Translated from the Japanese by Ryan C. K. Choi

The following, as the reader will see, are unedited notes. I have left them as such since I did not have the time or the emotional means to do anything more. However, even in rough form, these words are not without value.

September 14, 1923

A folk lute teacher—residence in Honjo-Yokoamichō, Tokyo— his name is Daifu Kane—age sixty-three—lives with his seventeen-year-old granddaughter—

House survives initial quake—neighborhood erupts in flames—they escape to Ryōgoku—no belongings except their parrot in his cage—parrot's name is Gorō—Gorō's back is gray—his belly is pink—his only tricks are mimicking the sound of a jeweler's

1. The 1923 Great Kantō earthquake.

mallet striking metal, and shrieking *"I see!"*—which sounds rather like *"Icee!"*—

Fleeing to Ningyōchō from Ryōgoku, he gets separated from his granddaughter—people in a frenzy—mountains of bags—no time to search—he sees a middle-aged lady with her caged canary—dressed like a brothel mistress—"I see there's someone else like me"—time still for banter and grins—

Arrives in Yoroibashi—half the neighborhood ablaze—heat so intense he feels his face broiling—raining debris—lead pipes covering the electrical wires melt, fall—people duck and dodge, jostle against him and Gorō in his cage—cage stays intact—Gorō tirelessly raves *"Icee! Icee!"*—

Arrives in Marunouchi—Imperial Theater, Police HQ scorched—a titanic pillar of smoke above Hibiya blots out the sky—he sees the bronze statue of Kusunoki, goes to sit on the lawn, stands—paces—sits, stands—goes to shout his granddaughter's name among the evacuees—sunset—he lays in the shadow of a pine next to a stockbroker and his office staff—smoke thickens in the sky—everywhere he looks, crimson—Gorō in his cage, *"Icee! Icee!"*—

Morning—resumes his search—Marunouchi first—then Hibiya—not Ryōgoku or Ningyōchō—"I didn't want to return there"—noon—hunger—searing thirst—he drinks water from Hibiya Pond—his granddaughter nowhere to be found—sunset—back to Marunouchi—he lays on the lawn, head propped on Gorō's cage so no one steals him—he remembers the people at the pond catching the ducks with their hands and eating them alive—he stares at the lights from the fire in the sky—

Day Three—abandons his search—journeys to Shinjuku to

find his nephew—en route from Sakurada to Hanzōmon he hears
Shinjuku is burning too—he reroutes to Yanaka—the family
temple is there—he looks at Gorō and thinks of the ducks—"I
can't kill Gorō," he tells himself, "but if he dies, I'll eat him to
survive"—next, Kudan-ue—government workers distributing raw
rice—he takes his scoop, eats it uncooked—Gorō watches from
his cage—"*Icee! Icee!*"—worrying that the squawks will be a nui-
sance at the temple he feeds Gorō the last of the rice—frees him on
the banks of the canal—sunset—arrives in Yanaka—the temple is
there—the priest welcomes him in—

On the morning of the fifth day, Daifu knocked on my door,
with no news of his granddaughter's fate. He was so haggard that I
didn't recognize the spirited teacher that I've always known.

*

Coda: Daifu's nephew's house in Shinjuku was spared. After their
separation, his granddaughter had found shelter there

Hat and Bonnie

Chelsea Hodson

I wanted a dog more than anything in the world. As a child, I resented my friends who seemed to take their dogs for granted. I longed for a pet that could learn tricks, cuddle, sleep in my bed. But in a suburb of Phoenix, Arizona, I'd turn and look through the sliding glass doors that opened to our backyard, and I'd see tortoises and turtles making their way across the landscape. They were so scaly and dry, so prehistoric and dumb. I often wondered why my parents kept turtles at all. When asked, my parents would say something about our pets being "low maintenance," since they only had to be fed once a day and they hibernated in the winter.

"Dog" was my first word, and I was obsessed for my entire childhood. I had a subscription to *Dog Fancy* magazine, and I spent many school lunch hours in the library, memorizing breeds in a dog encyclopedia. Instead of playing outside with my friends, I preferred to stay indoors imagining dogs. I think that says a lot about how I became a writer, actually. When I asked my mother recently about my childhood obsession, she described me as "always on a campaign to get a dog." I begged and pleaded, but my mother's allergies to cats and dogs were no match for my desire, and it broke both of our hearts.

Instead, we had between twenty and thirty desert tortoises and box turtles in our backyard at any given time. My parents had adopted a few from an animal sanctuary, and I named them after things they reminded me of: Hat, and Bonnet (who we referred to as Bonnie). This duo populated the backyard year after year until the joke went that, if the desert tortoise, an endangered species, was ever announced extinct, we could contact someone to let them know they actually weren't extinct. Each year, my mom found up to fifteen new baby tortoises roaming around the yard. Sometimes we'd give them all away. Sometimes we'd keep a few.

It was easy to see why desert tortoises were endangered. I couldn't imagine them in the wild at all. They seemed totally inept, like children, meandering at a glacial pace, eating anything that looked like food. If you picked one up, it might pee out of fear, and die shortly thereafter of dehydration. If it tipped itself over trying to climb over a rock or a tree root, it could spend hours trying to get right side up and still not make it. Their shells were cumbersome, and their long digging claws were dull from the dirt. Their bodies seemed ancient and fragile. Their extinction seemed imminent, and yet their survival seemed miraculous when I really thought about it: the most boring of dinosaurs had survived.

Playing with them was out of the question. They weren't entirely afraid of humans—probably because they knew we were the ones who put out leftover lettuce, melon rinds, and frozen vegetables for them to eat every day. So, I could touch a tortoise's shell without any reaction, but when I touched its head or its feet, it would kind of shudder, as if preparing to die. And I was mildly afraid of Hat after seeing what he was capable of during mating season—he'd chase Bonnie around the yard, bobbing his head vigorously, sometimes biting her legs until she was bleeding, then mounting her when she finally gave in. It was a horror show, and I closed the blinds whenever it happened.

I don't remember naming any of the box turtles, probably because they never stuck around long enough for me to be able to differentiate one from the other. They defied the turtle stereotype and sprinted across the yard, which always kind of creeped me out. They could swim in water, and they also weren't totally vegetarian—they ate dog food with meat in it, which seemed disgusting to me. There was something about their amphibian omnivorous nature that didn't sit right with me—as if evolution hadn't made up its mind yet.

I preferred the desert tortoises, with their dinner-plate bodies and their eighty-year life expectancy. Hat and Bonnie and some of the others came up to the house every day at five in the afternoon, pawing at the sliding glass doors. They kept some kind of internal clock, which told them when they were about to be fed, and if we were late, they came to remind us. It was the closest to a dog I was going to get, which depressed me whenever I thought about it.

In a plexiglass cage in our living room, my parents had one other pet: Fluffy, the Mexican red-knee tarantula. There are photos of me holding her in my hands: I guess that's how desperate I was. Despite her predatory ability to trap and devour live crickets, Fluffy was a gentle creature that tiptoed her hairy legs up my arm until it was time to put her away again. Once a year, she would molt so efficiently and delicately that her entire old exoskeleton would remain intact. It was shocking whenever we looked inside after she had molted: it looked as if she had cloned herself. Tarantulas and tortoises might have seemed exotic to my friends, but, to me, they were just an ordinary collection of shells and exoskeletons and other barriers that kept us apart.

To be a child is to be a student of longing: I was learning how to live without getting what I wanted. I was petting the scaly heads of tortoises that recoiled from my touch, I was letting a tarantula discover me, and I was always, forever dreaming of the dog I couldn't have.

FRANKIE

Kristen Iskandrian

Let the record show that I wanted a cat. I understood cats, inso-
far as I understood that they defied all understanding. To understand a cat is a trespass. They exist as a counterpoint to human
need, whereas dogs exist as hyperboles of human need. I dislike
hyperbole.

Let the record show that I didn't even want a cat, not really. I
wanted a third baby, not a pet.

Let the record show that I consciously avoid prose and poetry
about pets. I don't want to read about an animal being someone's
unlikely sage or savior. An impatience growls in me; I want to get
to the people, what the people are doing to one another. When an
animal is the main character I feel cheated.

But here I am, the owner of a terrier-mutt named Frankie, who
lives in our house with the rest of us, a member of the family, a
main character. We first saw Frankie inside the Humane Society's

mobile unit in the parking lot of the public library. He looked—
still does—like a cross between a fox and a deer. He seemed very
timid and did not bark, not that day, and not a day later, when we
spent more time with him at the Humane Society, petting him
and giving him treats. He hopped right up onto our laps, grateful
for any attention, affectionate. I'm convinced that I left my body
during those two days, days in which we decided that we would be
taking him home. I was two people: the person who felt apathet-
ic-verging-on-disdainful about dogs, who prized cleanliness and
order above most things, who treasured her quiet and solitude, who
hated bad smells, who, if anything, was a *cat person*; and the person
who'd just adopted a dog.

LET THE RECORD show that the kids were elated. They adored
him then and they adore him now, even if on occasion they lament
that he's not "fluffier," "chubbier," "better," "less annoying."

We adopted Frankie and then went to Oregon for a week, so we
weren't able to bring him home right away. When we picked him
up for good, he came bounding out to meet us, ears back, tongue
flapping wildly, paws skidding all over the waxed floors. He peed
a giant golden puddle of delight, which everyone thought was en-
dearing and hilarious. Everyone but me. My heart sank like Wile
E. Coyote off a cliff with an Acme anvil attached to his leg. *What
have I done. What have I permitted.*

Two days after we brought him home, Frankie (née Paco) discovered his bark. It was sharp, loud, and continuous. I felt something more intense than buyer's remorse but probably less serious
than postpartum depression, a despair that sapped my energy and

whittled my patience and made me snap at my non-barking, non-offensive children. Some weeks passed during which we blundered around, consulting pet websites and Cesar Millan books, spending a lot of money on new dog beds and harness leashes and anti-bark collars and fancy food. People say "adopt don't shop," which is great and everything, but pound dogs are far from free. Often, they are puzzles that most well-meaning people will go to great lengths and expense to try to solve. Their sad pasts are known or guessed at—he was abandoned so has anxiety, he was beaten so learned to bite—but the reality is that they are wild, descendants of wolves, with instincts that have been blunted and bastardized from all the inbreeding and cross-breeding, and most of us lack the skills or time or money to figure out exactly how to keep them happy.

LET THE RECORD show that we didn't know what we were doing, and nothing we did worked. After he'd destroyed a few things, made enough noise to draw the neighbors' ire more than a couple of times, peed and shit all over the house, nipped at the kids and bit me twice, we enrolled in a one-day intensive family training course with a dog trainer, Peggy, who was, at just under five feet tall and at least two across, the most intimidating person I have ever met. *The dog is the dog,* she told us. *It's you who have to be trained.* I was riveted, practically in love. Some people just have a way of snapping the world into focus. She eyed me scornfully. *Cute yes,* she said, *but certainly not a family dog.* Peggy told us everything that we had been doing wrong, which was everything: the way we held the leash, the tone of our voices when we gave commands, the rampant permissiveness. When Peggy walked with Frankie in slow, deliberate circles around the training room, he stayed right beside her, didn't pull or tarry. She told us he must never be allowed on the couch until we explicitly told him "it's okay," thereby inviting him up. She told us that every dog was desperate for a master, and if we didn't behave like masters, we would become the dogs, and Frankie would make the rules. I have since fantasized about hiring Peggy as my own personal warlock, because it seemed to me that there was nothing she couldn't do, nothing that scared or overwhelmed her, nothing she couldn't materially change with one slight pivot of her thick wrist. One time, dropping Frankie off for his weekly continuing ed, which we signed him up for at her behest and which he still does, I saw her get out of a Porsche followed by three Dobermans. I feel as though Peggy should be the most famous person in the world, and I think she feels that way, too.

LET THE RECORD show that we also secured and filled a Prozac prescription for Frankie, which I have thought about dipping into more than once. It's a tiny dose, the smallest, and we give it to him on a spoonful of peanut butter every afternoon. I find it amusing that, to him, the taste of peanut butter and the reality of that blue pill are forever linked, that in his mind, it's the pill that's delivering the peanut butter.

It has been three long years. My husband and I will look at each other in the evenings after the kids are asleep, Frankie curled up between us on the couch as we scroll through Netflix, and one or the other of us will say something like "he's such a good boy" or "he's really become a great dog." And then, like clockwork, a day or three later, he'll barf all over the rug or devour our entire dinner or bark unceasingly at the dryer or snarl at a baby. And I'll wish I could just drive him out to the woods or find out where Peggy lives and dump him on her doorstep. *Sorry, kids. I guess he just ran away. You know he was always a little crazy.* I picture their tearstained faces and feel—God forgive me—nothing.

LET THE RECORD show that Frankie answers to any and all of the following: Frank, Frankie, Francis, Saint Francis, Franklin, Franklin Delano Roosevelt, Frankles, boy-boy, baby, Mister Man, Mister Baby-Man, Doctor Mister Baby-Man.

Let the record show that I'm not a monster. I do understand, or at least I sort of understand, how and why some people love their pets as though they are children. I do not love Frankie as though he is my child. I'd kill for my children and die for my children, and I would do neither of those things for Frankie. My love for my children suffocates me at times; it's a force so powerful that it extends, in moments, into darkness. My joy in them outsizes me, like a rough sea that threatens to capsize my entire tiny life. *I'm just one person!* I want to yell. *How did these two people happen?* Theirs wasn't a love I had to learn. It predated them; it even predated me. It's a love that feels ancient and eternal.

But let the record show that, because of Frankie, I now believe in gradations of love, varietals of love. I now believe that commitment can come first, and love can follow. Like my grandmother used to say: when you don't enjoy doing something, you should do it more. I always considered love to be one thing, an enormously unchill thing. But maybe, I'm finding, love can be chill, can happen in glacially slow, incremental layers. Because of Frankie, I'm *learning to love.* With Frankie, I feel cautious and jilted and leery and mad. I feel bad at love. And yet, every day, it's the two of us: on walks, on the big chair, in the car, in the yard. At some point, I made him mine, or he made me his. It's a difficult, dawdling, non-instinctual, sometimes infuriating love, but it's there, becoming itself, different and specific. I feel it.

Magellan

David Nutt

The woman's apartment is one large experiment in argyle, from her diamond wallpaper to the lozenge-patterned curtains and same carpet to the woman's somber frock. Reinhart sits at her dinner table, mesmerized by all these jarring symmetries, unable to decide if the woman's schoolmarm garb is a costume after all, or maybe a private kink, an ironic affectation. He remembers his racquet-ball partner, Mitch Vitner, saying something about the woman—Patty? Patricia? Patrice?—being an educational administrator of some sort. Then again, Mitch also told Reinhart he was invited to a party. A *costume* party. Reinhart showed up on the woman's doorstep dressed in a rented astronaut suit, ungainly sized and humpy, that he augmented at home with tinfoil and PVC and tape to add some retro-futuristic flair. There was no party on the premises. Just the woman, her staid outfit, a candlelit dinner for two.

"How's it feel to be set up?" she asked, opening the door wide.

"Do you feel like a chump? Because *I* feel like a chump. If I knew Neil Armstrong was coming over to my condo, I would've buried the bodies and hidden the hacksaws."

The meal is some type of leafy vegan concoction that Reinhart studies with meek suspicion. The woman smiles often, too often, an effort that involves the whole terrain of her face. Her ears redden, her eyes disappear in a squint. She is smiling so hard her face has turned several malevolent shades of pinot noir. Reinhart, for his part, stares straight ahead, chewing his forage with dark industriousness, trying not to wince or twitch too much. He's barely able to ambulate in his costume. He listens to her with the motionless intensity of a Portuguese water dog awaiting table scraps.

"I'm sorry I don't have any Tang for us to drink," she says.

"Tang?"

"The space drink. Don't you remember the commercials? There was a whole marketing gimmick in the '70s. Like that kitschy song about the sad polysexual astronaut stranded in his spinning tin can."

"It's just a costume," he replies. "Mitch said this was supposed to be—"

"I know, right?" She dabs a garlic bread slab into the butter bowl, and some collateral spatter is flung onto Reinhart's expensive suit sleeve. He glares at it and licks, licks, licks until it is gone.

"Isn't it sorta funny how no one seems to want to go to space anymore?" she asks. "I guess once they start sending up Border Collies and Canadians, you know it's a tired scene. Not that I don't adore Canadians."

Reinhart wants to shrug but shrugging his suit requires an extensive system of locomotion. Instead, he sits and nods, blinking away a tide of sweat that gushes from the far peak of his shrinking hairline. He can feel his whole forehead shimmer and flare.

"Does that thing have a built-in commode?" she asks.

"The lady at the costume store asked me the same thing," Reinhart replies in a shy, chapped voice. "But I don't know. I haven't tried to go to the bathroom yet."

"Mysterious," she nods.

Reinhart stabs at the green pile on his plate in a congenial manner. He's trying to avoid glancing at the open bedroom door immediately behind him, a blood-red light leaking out.

"That's a funny thing about astronauts," the woman says. "They have to maintain a purity of body and spirit, steely discipline. All that time stoically floating around the cosmos, racking up medals, footwear endorsements, cereal box sponsorships. Then you realize all these space heroes are whizzing down the leg of their million-dollar suits. Some role models. Mitch says you're a real zealot about your racquetball."

"I like racquetball," Reinhart semi-shrugs. "How do you know Mitch?"

"He's Robby's dad."

"Who is Robby?"

"I teach first grade. Robby is one of my wards. The kids are brilliant, truly they are, but sometimes I step back and look at them and all I see are future bank presidents, sorority treasurers, bail bondsman, and hemophiliacs. It makes me wonder how much damage I'm actually doing. To them and myself."

She tries to smile again, but this time she doesn't flash much tooth or gum line at him. Just a rootless melancholy that causes Reinhart to sweat even more. He leans closer to pretend to hear.

The sudden tilt makes his suit slosh.

"Mitch said he wanted to introduce us because both of us are lame and single and disastrously unmarryable," she says. "Is that true? Are you disastrously unmarryable?"

"Well, I don't—"

"I'm sorry, but quiet sweaty men make me nervous. Mitch says he can sniff the lonely burning off you like fog. I thought that was a rather lofty poeticism."

"Mitch is okay," Reinhart says, which is only a half lie. The man is definitely named Mitch.

"He and his wife sort of adopted me," the woman says. "They're not very nice people, but I guess I'm not a very nice orphan. And I don't have many social options out here in the boonies. I used to have a sister. I don't see her anymore. She joined some kind of desert fitness cult. Have you heard about these things? A tribe of gainfully employed men and women drive out to Utah, squeeze into some spandex, and they go running in the mountains and don't stop. Days, weeks, months. People keel over from dehydration, they lose their hair. They're born again. Sometimes they never come back."

"I've never heard of that."

"I didn't even know the flaky cult tramp *liked* running."

The woman sucks the last smear of butter from her bread wedge and flicks the crust down the open yawning neck of Reinhart's suit.

"Ten points," she says, both arms forked up. Field goal.

Reinhart cringes while trying to peer down the suit. He can't tell what is food, what is darkness, what is mangled wound. So he concentrates on shuttling the greenage from one side of his plate to the other, afraid the woman is scrutinizing him, itemizing him. Man. Mangle. Mangle. Man.

"Are you sure you don't want some wine?" she asks.

"I'm trying to abstain."

"You look like you've sweated half your body weight from that eggy forehead of yours."

"There's all this, this…" He struggles to lift a numb arm to indicate the candles and red light, an agonizing energy source somewhere askance of him, but he can't manage the movement. Some foreign temperature is irradiating his innards.

The woman reaches across the table and delicately pats his parka-puffed sleeve, which he cannot feel, either. "It would be a real shame if you drowned in this sucker before I had a chance to shovel you full of cheesecake."

After their meal, she walks him to her swank prefab sofa and supervises Reinhart's intricate docking procedure. Then she flicks a wall switch, and a fake fireplace in the corner of the room ignites. The argyle wallpaper crawls and throbs like living animal meat. Reinhart barely fits the sofa, nor the contours of his own mawing terror. She wedges in close against him, smiling bashfully, trying not to spill her fifth glass of wine as Reinhart continues his glacial melt all over her Scandinavian furniture.

The condominium is located on the forested fringe of town, adjacent to a sprawling land preserve. Reinhart keeps staring at the bay window, trying to glimpse the unruly nature on the far side of the pane, but he only sees his own expression—dark, slurry, terrified—staring back.

The woman runs a finger along his puffy arm seam. "What do you say I grab the chainsaw from my bedroom and cut you out of this thing?"

"I'm actually starting to like it," he replies. "I think it calms me."

"You're trying to abstain."

"Yes," he says.

"From drinking."

"Yes."

"Drugging."

"Yes."

"What about—"

"From everything," he blurts and accidentally glances at the blood-colored light expanding from the bedroom.

"I was going to say cha-cha dancing."

"That too."

She squirms herself through a series of postures and contortions, flat backed, whelked into a ball, legs curled under the sofa lip, unable to establish comfortable traction.

"All that anxiety, all that selfish devotion," she says. "Maybe you believe too much in the body."

"I don't think I do that."

"A few years ago, I had one of those IUD things grappling-hook'd in my uterus. But my insides spat the thing out, rejected it. It was as if I had shoved a uranium rock up there or something. It wasn't my fault. Our bodies are not honest places. We try to treat them kindly, but ultimately they betray us."

"Can I get a glass of water?" Reinhart asks.

"I know about your injury," she tells him.

"Seltzer. Tap water. Anything."

"Mitch warned me. He's seen you shriveling in the corner of the swampy locker room, trying to hide yourself, dressing in a hurry. Maybe that's what puts the handsome little halo over your head."

Reinhart tries not to flinch, tries not to wince. He has a

tremendous arsenal of facial tics at his disposal but little dominion over any of them.

"I don't know Mitch very well," he says. "The league organizer paired us up. He has horrendous B.O. He doesn't know what he's talking about."

"But the scar—"

"There's no scar," Reinhart snaps.

The woman sighs and tips her head back and regards the ceiling, also blood-colored, also argyle, or so it seems to Reinhart, who is trying to lean aside and artfully dry his face on a bolster pillow.

"I have all sorts of spooky scar tissue, too, stuffed up my insides," the woman says.

Reinhart stops mashing his face across the upholstery and rolls sideways, aiming his one good ear at her, actually listening now.

"I used to get these brain-buster migraines when I was a teenager," she says. "Real blinding, skull-crunching attacks. The hurt was so bad it must have done obscene damage to my internal parts. The wet organs and tubes and barnacles and the starchy wiring that holds together my starchy brain. You know how I know? One day, randomly, the migraines stopped. And I missed them. I really missed them. It's amazing, isn't it? Pain can be a holy thing."

Reinhart is about to speak when he startles at the sound, jerking forward, knocking wine everywhere.

"Did something just howl at us? Outside?"

"Oh that," she says, nonchalantly dabbing puddles with her frock. "That's my wolf."

Out the bay window, Reinhart sees the flat yard against a crust of forest, a rising dark. "A real wolf?"

"A lonely stray. I guess it got separated from the pack. Don't worry. I've got protection for that."

She reaches under the couch and comes up with a double-barrel shotgun, sale sticker still affixed. "Just in case the animal is rabid and I need to scare it, chase it off."

She swings the weapon around, presenting Reinhart with the broad oak stock. "Would you like to do the honors?"

Reinhart considers the gun, the yard, the dark. As she leans forward to nudge him with the weapon, Reinhart is granted an incidental view down the front of her sweater, black bra strap, steep cleavage.

"Make it back alive," she says, quickly closing up her sweater, "and we can pin a gold star on you."

Something flutters in the purple mangled wreckage of his loins. Reinhart grabs the gun and runs.

THE DARK IS held at bay by a single flood lamp aimed at the middle of the backyard. Into this circle Reinhart steps, gun at hip level, his free hand searching about his suit. He checks his marsupial pouch and, sure enough, a previous renter has left several raisins, a breath mint, and half a granola bar zipped into the lining. Reinhart crosses the forest threshold with the granola bar extended. The underbrush creaks. A chorus of secret wildlife chirps at him. He finds a length of rope around a tree, partial fixings from an abandoned hammock. Reinhart sets the shotgun on the forest floor and ties the snack food on the rope and slings the rope over a high branch and waits.

At the crunching of crispy leafage, Reinhart ignites the novelty penlight he keeps on his keychain and illuminates the low skulky approach of a rangy-legged coyote. The animal does not seem interested in the snack. It continues toward Reinhart with a relaxed and unblinking focus, its eyes a little watery, its body mostly bone. Reinhart slips the food from its rope and tries to feed the coyote by hand. The animal gives a few exploratory nibbles. Through the top tier of forest, Reinhart can almost see the schoolteacher's bedroom window. He shuts his eyes and imagines her standing there in some sort of furry mink gown that barely covers the kingdom of her sex. All along her thighs, a series of massive scars, dozens of them, jagged and latticed and thicketed, lush and red. The fantasy makes Reinhart lightheaded. A wave of blackout comes sailing forth across the horizon.

Then the harsh tongue strokes his outstretched palm, the coyote licking in concentric circles. The sensation drags Reinhart back to the safe, chaste confines of his suit. He rubs the animal's ears, tamps its long snout.

He loops the rope around the coyote's neck, and together Reinhart and the animal push deeper into the woods.

THEY ARE TRAVELLING a rural road plagued with ruts and potholes and rotten drainage. The nighttime is dreamily silent. Reinhart can only see a few dozen feet in front of him, but the landscape feels endless. He is reminded of green-pleated valleys and desert plains, lonely aquatic underworlds, a soundless cosmos looming above. Reinhart has never been much of a moony-eyed romantic about the sky or its stars. He harbors no great obsession with alien creations or mystical voids. He simply feels sheltered in the silence, the span, the vanishing.

He pauses in the middle of the road and regards the coyote on its leash.

"Magellan," Reinhart tells the animal. "You look exactly like a Magellan."

The coyote cocks its head, licks its stalagmite teeth, blinks.

"I was never allowed to have pets," Reinhart explains. "Just chemistry sets, model rockets. That's how I lost the finger and half my hearing when I was a kid. It's only part of a pinky, and if you're gonna lose one of the troops, that's the one to lose."

He raises his hand and flexes four-and-a-half digits. "I can't play the guitar well, either."

A pair of headlights blazes their way, and a car stops on the road's shoulder.

"Son," the older driver says. "Is that a coyote you are walking on a rope?"

"Yes, sir."

"Magnificent," the man replies.

Reinhart nods. The man nods back. The car resumes a sluggish pace, the driver staring at Reinhart and his animal via a rearview mirror strung with rosaries, Mardi Gras beads. Reinhart is still waving farewell in the middle of the road with his gently maimed hand, whispering gibberish to his coyote, when a speeding carload of teenagers shoots around the corner and mows him down.

THE ROOM IN which he wakes is not blood-colored at all. Everything is lit by Christmas lights, multihued and seizuring, stapled and vined along the seams of particleboard ceiling. The walls are painted pastel. The bed is a shoddy futon in a dank basement apartment without windows. A dozen teenagers mill around with red plastic cups they are trying to sip intelligently. The smell of stale keg beer permeates the bruised furniture, a seismic throbbing of dance music so loud it ruptures and distorts. Reinhart feels surprisingly fine. He feels elevated. He finds his broken arm is splinted with a rolled magazine and duct tape, his legs bloody and naked, shins imbedded with pebble shrapnel. He is sitting in his soiled underwear. Across the room, the coyote occupies a deflated beanbag chair, tongue aslant, contentedly panting away. A tall kid with train tracks shaved into his purple hair is wearing Reinhart's astronaut suit while another kid, same haircut in orange, snaps his picture with a camera phone.

"Got it," Orange Head says, then screams, "Next!"

An oafish girl in tribal dress, whalebone stabbed through her septum, helps shoehorn the tall kid loose and tries to squeeze herself into the suit. Reinhart can hear the sound of fake space-age nano-polymer fabric ripping apart, and he can't help it, the feeling overtakes him, and he flashes them a maniacal grin.

"Looks like the road kill is feeling better," Purple Head says. Nude and shaved hairless, he joins Reinhart on the futon and pumps his hand. "I'm Marcus, and these are my minions."

"Haaaaallo," Reinhart replies and waves at the room.

Marcus mimics the wave, then squints and grabs Reinhart's hand. "Fuck, dude. Did we run off part of your pinky?"

"I was born that way."

"Shit is harsh. Maybe the doc needs to up your dosage."

"Dosage?"

Marcus clambers to his feet, all lank and knocky knees and genitals swinging, and hollers, "Medic!"

An ordinary-looking kid with a stethoscope dangling from his throat wanders through the crowd. He's holding a jagged commando knife that he shoves under the futon mattress. Then he takes a knee and roves a flashlight around Reinhart's face. "Condolences. This one's been dead for days."

"Give him a little extra anyway. To take him across the river."

The ordinary kid holds Reinhart's hand open and shakes a vial over it. Six pills topple in. He neatly folds each of Rinehart's fingers over the stash. The partial pinky juts out, aloof.

Reinhart raises the fist near his face.

"But I abstain," he says in a baby boy voice.

"That's hilarious!" Marcus shouts. "This dude is hilarious!"

"We fixed that itch hours ago," Ordinary says as he fetches the hunting knife. "Had to medicate the shit out of you. Your dog, too."

"My dog?"

"That's why homeboy is armed," Marcus says. "Lassie tried to bite him."

Ordinary crawls over to the coyote with the knife in hand, pushing his face up to the animal's muzzle. "Good boy!" he screams.

The coyote doesn't flinch.

"Double dosage," Marcus nods. "A real miracle worker. You better put those magic beans away before someone nicks them. A lot of hungry mouths around this place tonight. Must be the full moon."

"Beans?"

"The pills, man."

"I don't take pills."

"You *already* took pills. Happy travels. First batch is on the house. Sell 'em. Pop 'em later. Whatever. Just so we're even-steven and shit about running you over. I don't need any more points on my license."

Reinhart feels the room crowding with pale, steaming bodies, and he wants to rise, step forth, sermonize. But his limbs are sludged. He coaxes his eyes towards Marcus.

"Is this a Halloween party?"

"I dunno. What's Halloween?" Marcus leans into the crowd and shouts: "Anybody know what the fuck Halloween is?"

Just shrugs. Blank looks.

Even though he is no longer wearing the suit, Reinhart is still having a difficult time navigating his own body. He can't quite get all the pulleys and levers and silly string that control his appendages to cooperate, but there is some voltage there, some swing and stretch.

"I want to say something to your friends," he says.

"No friends here. Only freaks, frauds, and beauty queens."

"I want to debrief them."

"About what?"

"My story."

"They know your story, brother. You're the Saddest Ever Astronaut. You wear the crown."

"But I feel great. Really, really great."

Marcus takes careful hold of Reinhart's head, tips it back, and funnels the beer down Reinhart's open throat.

Reinhart spasms, gags. The beer spews back out from his blowhole in a thick cetacean mist that elicits a boisterous rugby cheer from the room. Someone claps his back. Someone shakes him. Reinhart angles his head towards the heavens and yelps: "Purity of body keeps the astronaut afloat!"

A group of skinheads in monochrome tunics nod sagely and take up the chant. "Purity of body keeps the astronaut afloat! Purity of body keeps the astronaut afloat!" Soon the whole room is singing, and someone has gripped Reinhart under the armpits and lifted him to his feet.

"Tell us about your dog," a skinhead says.

"He's my coyote," Reinhart says. "He had a name. I can't remember the name."

"There's a truth in that, man."

"I like your head," Reinhart says and licks the kid's shorn scalp. The kid allows it. "The coyote has a story. A really important story."

The skinheads and haircolors and twitchy addicts surround Reinhart in pious assembly. Someone has muted the music. The volume in Reinhart's head goes way up.

"The young coyote went to outer space once," Reinhart says. "He was part of an experimental government program. They put him in a glass bubble and catapulted him into the heavens, but he got lost—so lost, in fact, he mislaid years of his life—just floating around, staring out the porthole at the empty slough of space. The heavens didn't want him, you understand? He plummeted back to suburban Earth, a slightly older, less agile coyote, and limped away from the wreckage without any gripe or grievance. He got a decent job and a studio apartment that didn't depress him too much, a discount gym membership. But he still felt he was sealed inside that glass bubble, still rolling across the infinite murk. One day at work, he was putzing around the lab, not paying attention, not sober either, because he had a habit of saturating his breakfast cereal with Kahlua and vodka and crumbled pain pills because he hadn't much talent at abstaining from anything. Maybe he was scared of losing that faraway feeling. He inadvertently mixed the wrong lab samples. There was a fast explosion. The coyote suffered an atrocious chemical burn upon a sensitive area of his coyote body. The doctors called it a disfigurement. The crazy thing is, the accident didn't change much about his life. The coyote still went to work. He still ate lunch in his car. Some days, he sits in this car, chewing his turkey-and-artichoke sandwich, looking across the parking lot at the other coyotes sitting in *their* cars, eating *their* turkey-and-artichoke sandwiches, and all the world's sadness finally starts to make sense. It almost doesn't feel sad at all. That's how the story ends."

"So it's a bummer ending?"

"It's the happiest ending there is," Reinhart replies. "Everyone survived."

The shaved heads nod. Drinks are conscientiously sipped.

"Welp," Marcus sighs. "It's not gonna be a happy ending for this coyote, I'm afraid."

Reinhart nods his head knowingly, then freezes. "Wait, I'm sorry, what?"

"Your dog, man. Guess the medicine didn't agree with him."

Reinhart stumbles through the crowd and finds the coyote sagged over the side of its beanbag, tongue loose and purple, a frozen rictus grin.

"Oh," Reinhart says. "Oh, oh, oh."

He falls to the floor and scoops up the animal's head, which has seemingly gained dozens of pounds in death, its fur bristlier, its skin no longer pulsating with heat. Reinhart heaves the limp coyote into his lap and hugs it, holds it, won't let go.

"Blast off," Marcus says and signs the cross on the coyote's forehead, then strolls away.

The music kicks back on, but Reinhart can't hear it. He's stroking the animal's cold fur, squeezing up its final dribbles of life, or the first drips of death. Whatever unknowable substance fills the animal body after the spirit has been flushed free.

Reinhart looks up.

"He had a good name," he announces to all these people who do not hear him, who no longer realize he is in the room. "A really meaningful name."

Because his arm is pulverized and splinted, Reinhart can't carry the coyote far. So he rummages a pile of outdoor recreational equipment stored under the staircase and finds a child-sized toboggan, loads the coyote on it, and drags the toy through the party without drawing any notice, except that of a densely freckled young woman wearing the bottom half of Reinhart's space suit. Her top half is naked. Only a pair of Day-Glo skulls have been painted on her breasts.

"Ooh, look at that," she says in a songbird voice, pointing at the purple-velvety scar tissue that creeps up from Reinhart's elastic underwear band, flowering across his abdomen. "Is that sexy eggplant contagious?"

Reinhart is sobbing too hard to reply. He continues pulling his funeral sled through the mudroom and out the backdoor.

The house is located in a posh suburban subdivision that Reinhart doesn't recognize as he stands on the sidewalk, shivering violently in his underwear. The street names are unfamiliar, the landscape flat and otherworldly and blank. It could be anywhere, everywhere. He drags the toboggan down the middle of the road with his one good arm, no cars in sight, no pedestrians, the toboggan's wood bottom noisily chuffing the asphalt. The empty road connects to another empty road and then another and another. Reinhart struggles along, his lungs full of ice and brackish pond scum, the heavenly chemicals fading from his blood a little. Soon the chemicals are gone entirely. His sweet bliss goes with them. All that remains is sweeter punctured pain.

In this raw delirium, Reinhart fantasizes about returning to the schoolteacher's condo, stumbling through the door, collapsing in her argyle lap. He wants to apologize for his cowardly exit. He wants to nod eagerly at her panicked conversation and express gratitude for the fine vegetarian cuisine. At the very least, he wants to thank her for not stuffing his stomach with narcotics and killing the beautiful animal he is now towing across the countryside in some sort of morbid reverse Iditarod. But he can't find her condo, or anything vaguely condo-like, in this wilderness. The woman is slowly rolling away from him, he knows, in a befogged capsule, perhaps, too many miles and light-years and dead coyotes between them now. Too many mislaid lives.

Instead, after a long stretch of fallow acreage, he comes to the farmhouse. Whoever lives on the property has spent significant coinage trying to expunge the agrarian character. The barn has been bulldozed, the cattle pen dismantled, a tennis court added to the backyard with a motion-sensor light illuminating its pristine, unpainted surface. He looks at it, all of it. Reinhart parks his toboggan on the small margin of remaining yardage and crawls underneath a solitary picnic table, brand new, freshly weatherproofed. He pulls the dead coyote under the table with him and curls his

achy limbs around it. The stiff shape, the prickly fur, a strange synthetic smell. Reinhart nuzzles the wholeness. He clings the coarse
contours and swirled grain of a life that is now a dream. This is
how the homeowner will find them. Or maybe the schoolteacher, a
policeman, a team of government scientists, a cult of drug-hungry
pagans or saints. Reinhart and his coyote, their bodies knitted in
a clumsy embrace, damaged and exiled, alive and dead, tumbling
through the cosmos together.

Rainbow

Precious Okoyomon

After my parents got divorced my mother started dating a younger
man
She said she was tired of feeling bad she wanted to feel good and
appreciated
They met at the gym / he helped her lift her weights
He had recently come back from the war and didn't look anyone
in the eyes
They slowly fell into the plot of a good lifetime movie
They got matching tattoos
They got matching cars
They got a toy poodle together from my aunt the gynecologist
who breeds show poodles in her basement.

**HAPPINESS HAPPENS QUICKLY / SIMULATED
PERFECT REALITY COMING QUICK**

My mother named the dog after her boyfriend Andron
My mother declared he was a special dog and that he needed to be
treated with extra care
He needed to wear a diaper and eat eggs and bacon for every meal
My mother always acquired pets at random
She couldn't love them in a way that was good for them
Something bad always happened to them, as if she wished it upon
them
In my childhood we had

2 standard poodles that my mother gave away
10 chickens that my father ate
1 turtle that ran away
7 ducks that my father ate
4 rabbits that my father left in the parking lot of our local brunch
spot
4 hamsters that my mother let go
1 bird that flew away
1 cat that my father let go
1 goat that my father ate
10 fish that all ate each other / the last one died of depression

This new dog was special
My mother treated him like a baby
He seemed to be holding her together in her fragile state

Andron the poodle became a deliverance for our family
It was like we couldn't remember life without our poodle
We would sit around taking turns feeding him eggs and rice

mashed into a fine paste
My father had been gone for 3 months
No one talked about him
The encasing halo of loss is funny / the depression that comes
with abandonment / you sink into the endless body of the world
signaling at the liquidated border of your reality

My mother started taking antidepressants and buying Gucci for
the toy poodle

My mother started wearing less and going out more with her toy
poodle

He became a beacon of hope / her children and her marriage had
failed but she had a toy poodle named after her 27-year-old lover
Andron / she was blissful she was happy

**Death to loss!! Death to fear!! Death to the nuclear family!!
Death to dog shows!!**

Death to failure!! Death to all bad fathers!!

**Free the toy poodles of the world!! Free ur–suffering mother!!
Free Cesar Millan!!**

But the poodle was suffering
My mother forgot to walk the toy poodle
My brother never walked the poodle because he was depressed
and smoking weed

My mother's 27-year-old boyfriend couldn't walk the dog because
he hated the poodle and would lock him in a cage only feeding
him bologna from Walmart
I was too far from my family and my life and the toy poodle that
would save us all

One day in the frenzied sun of a soft summer my brother left the
poodle outside in his starry pothead state

So Andron the toy poodle ran away

He ran looking for salvation from my family

Looking for a place to not be worshiped past the bliss of sunlight's
wrenching maws

The loss of the object of love's distortion makes a person suscepti-
ble to madness

So my mother lost her mind in the ceaseless chaos of the world

So I came home from college to help my family find the toy
poodle

So my family would not fall into the sun spiral

Straight sucking on sadness

    My mother believed her beloved toy poodle dead

Flat
  Splat
Sprawled

Out in the street

So I made posters

So I made T-shirts

So I asked every neighbor

So I asked every flower

So I asked every child

Have you see the toy poodle? that will save us all

You will be surprised by who you become looking for your savior

The pain of separation makes you desperate

A neighbor told my brother someone down the street had found
an apricot toy poodle

  And took it to a shelter

My mother and I go to the shelter together

We are silent and the only song my mom has on the mixtape her boyfriend made her is playing on repeat loop after loop of "Over the Rainbow"

Have you ever heard the sound that a hummingbird makes when it's run over by a red BMW on its way to pick up a runaway toy poodle?

it's like an exploding heart

Your body feels like it's being strung along a harp's soundboard

Play that song again on the transformed material of you

Play my heart again on repeat

She doesn't notice the hummingbird or my heartbeat

The sky goes from light blue to lavender to pink before setting into cream and blue

At the shelter Andron the poodle
  seems resentful and afraid of my mother
He does not go to her when she calls him

BROKEN HEARTS DON'T HEAL SO QUICK / FOOL ME ONCE SHAME ON YOU! SHAME!

He comes to me

He sits in my lap

I hold him in my arms

I kiss him

I sing him "Over the Rainbow" on repeat

Apparitional love in fluorescent light

I don't let him go

On the drive home

I tell my mother renaming him is probably a good idea
Andron doesn't really fit him
He's more special than that
I sing him "Over the Rainbow" over and over again until he
becomes my rainbow

LIGHT THAT OPENS UP AND BECOMES A HEART

MIDGET

Scott McClanahan

1.

I was more afraid of Midget the Chihuahua than anything in the world. She was my great-aunt Nell's dog, and she used to sit on Nell's lap or sit by Nell's feet and snap at people as they walked by. One day, when I was a baby, Nell and my mom drove down to McDowell County to see Aunt Mollie. Aunt Mollie had a wooden leg, and she was embarrassed by the way the wooden leg looked and embarrassed by the way the wooden leg creaked and embarrassed by the way she limped when she took steps with her wooden leg and walked. We all sat down in Mollie's living room and that's when Midget went crazy.

Midget charged up to the wooden leg and showed her teeth. Aunt Mollie looked frightened and unsure what to do. She covered her wooden leg with a quilt, but Midget barked and growled and gnashed at it. Midget bit and snapped and her teeth echoed against the wood. Aunt Mollie looked afraid to move and tried to kick

Midget away. My mom held me in her arms and finally said, "Nell, you need to get that dog out of here." Midget snarled and snapped, "Motherfuckers. Motherfuckers. I'll kill you all."

Nell laughed and said, "Oh, she's just scared of that horrible wooden leg is all. I'm kind of scared of it too."

My mom saw Mollie blush and bow her head, embarrassed at the words "wooden leg."

When my mom tells this story now, she says, "You know Aunt Mollie had a hard life. Lost her husband in the mines and her only daughter committed suicide and you know it must have embarrassed her, her wooden leg being talked about that way."

But Midget wasn't done that day. My mom put me down on the floor, and for some reason baby Scott made Midget nervous and she started growling. She lunged like she was going to attack. She growled and snapped and gritted her teeth just a few inches from my face. My mom picked me up and held me, scared. Then Midget went back to the wooden leg and growled at it again.

My mom and Mollie looked back and forth at each other, but Nell didn't say anything about Midget. My mom was mad now and shouted and kicked at the dog.

"Get out of here, Midget." She looked at my great-aunt Nell who was drinking a coke and eating a candy bar and who didn't say anything. My mom said, "You keep that dog away from my baby, Nell." My great-aunt Nell picked Midget up in her arms and laughed. She said, "Oh it's okay, Midget. You're just trying to protect me, aren't you? That old wooden leg and that mean baby are making you afraid. Poor baby." She hugged Midget, and my mom went into the other room disgusted.

Midget growled, "That's right, motherfuckers. I'll kill you all."

2.

When I was a little boy, we went to a nice restaurant with Nell and she ordered a hamburger but didn't eat any of it. My mom asked, "Is something wrong with your food?"

My great-aunt Nell said, "Oh no. I was just thinking about Midget."

My mom and dad and I finished eating and the waitress came up and noticed Nell wasn't eating anything. "Is something wrong with your food, darling?"

Nell said, "No, I just ordered food so I could take this home to my dog."

The waitress said, "Okay, a whole hamburger?"

My mom said, "Well maybe you should try and eat a little, Nell."

Nell said no. She would have a candy bar later for dinner. Then she reached inside her purse and started searching for something.

My mom said, "Nell, we can get you a box and maybe you can eat some of it later. Those candy bars aren't healthy for dinner."

But Nell said, "Oh no. It's fine. I brought some cheese wrappers." She pulled out ten or twelve of the greasy used cheese wrappers that slices of cheese came in then. Nell tore up the hamburger and wrapped the chunks in the greasy cheese paper. The waitress walked away confused. My mom and dad and I watched her putting the new food in old food wrappers and then placing them back into her purse.

When we got home, Midget sniffed at the hamburger but didn't even eat it. That night, before we went to bed, my dad said, "I didn't know I was buying dinner for a little shit-ass Chihuahua who tries to bite everybody."

My mom said, "One day that dog is going to hurt somebody. You just wait."

3.

Then it happened. My aunt Jean was in the kitchen at Nell's house in Baltimore. Nell was in the bedroom. Jean was getting something to drink, and Midget followed her. I was sitting at the counter, reading an old newspaper article about the Baltimore Orioles. Jean dropped a paper towel on the floor, and Midget took off charging from the corner of the kitchen and attacked.

Jean tried to pull her hand back from the paper towel, but Midget's teeth cut into her skin. She cried out. Jean looked at her mangled hand and kicked at Midget. And then we saw the blood coming down.

The thumb skin was torn open in a tiny tear and pulled back jagged. The thumb meat was showing and exposed. Nell came into the kitchen and said, "Oh god, what did you do?"

Jean stood there bleeding and said, "What did I do? I dropped a paper towel and your spoiled-ass Chihuahua just bit me."

Nell picked Midget up and held her tight. "Oh Midget, are you okay? Did she scare you?"

Jean washed the bloody bite off in the sink and said, "I'm the one who got bit."

My great-aunt Nell shook her head and rolled her eyes. "Well I don't know why you're complaining that much. Midget has had all her shots. She just nipped you a little bit, anyway."

Then my mom took my aunt Jean to the doctor.

When Jean got home with her bandaged-up hand, she wanted revenge. So that afternoon when Nell went to the store to get a new roast beef, after Jean showed her the freezer burn covering the old one, my aunt Jean caught Midget upstairs in Nell's bedroom and said, "Do you remember me, Midget? I'm the one who you fucked with today." Then Jean charged Midget, fast like a monster, and shouted, "Argghh," with her arms up flailing. Midget barked afraid, but Jean kept going until suddenly Midget changed. Midget was shaking and scared.

"I'm going to fucking kill you. You little shit dog. That crazy-ass old woman isn't here to protect your ass now."

Midget took off running. Jean chased her down the steps and then into the kitchen and then back up the steps and into the bed-room, screaming and shrieking all the way. Midget pissed a tiny puddle and it glistened on the hardwood floors.

Jean caught her by the back of the neck in the upstairs hallway and held her down hard. Midget wasn't trying to snap or bite or growl anymore. She just wanted to submit. Jean picked her up and walked to the edge of the stairs, carrying Midget like a bowling ball, letting her swing back and forth.

"Oh what's that, Midget? You want to go on a little rocket ride?" By this time Grandma Audrey and my mom came out of their rooms to watch with me. Jean swung Midget back one last time and then threw the dog down the stairs.

Midget sailed and skidded and bounced against the ground floor and then bounced back again. Midget sat for a second and then took off, scared. She gave me a look as she passed me at the kitchen door: "That bitch is crazy, Scott. That crazy bitch is trying to kill me." Midget left a tiny piss river behind her on the way to the kitchen closet.

And then my mom and grandma applauded. I applauded too because it had come to pass that Midget was our tormentor no more.

She had been broken by the real bitch. My aunt Jean.

But after Jean left, Midget only got meaner and more possessive of Nell. The day after she bit Jean, Midget cornered me in a room. I needed to pee, but the bathroom was directly behind where Midget was sitting, and she growled at me.

I tried to move but Midget watched me and snarled. She was on one side and I was on the other side, trapped. I stood for a long time needing to pee while my mom and Nell talked. My face started making funny shapes and I couldn't hold it anymore.

My mom finally said, "What's wrong, Scott?"

I started to cry and whispered to her what was wrong. I held myself and bounced a few times. I wiped the tears that popped from my eyes with my tiny fist. My mom said, "Well, Scott, don't cry. Let's go use the bathroom. It's okay."

She led me past Midget and we walked into Nell's bathroom. I pulled up the toilet seat but then I felt something bust. I heard a spray and felt the warm water soaking my underwear and rolling down my leg. I looked at the floor and there were little tributaries of pee spreading across the tile. I cried some more, embarrassed, and Mom said, "It's okay. Don't get upset. Don't let an old dog keep you from using to the bathroom, Scott."

4.

And so in the years to come, Midget grew old. I was twelve now and Midget didn't scare me anymore. She walked slower and whined like she was in pain. She couldn't even hop on the couch to sit on Nell's lap because her arthritis was so bad. Her tiny Chihuahua legs were covered and bunched in knots. And Nell's attention was no longer on Midget but two new dogs—Samantha and Nanook.

Samantha was a collie with warm brown eyes. Nanook was a giant white mutt who chewed up everything and who was always stealing Midget's toys and destroying them.

Midget watched Sam and me playing fetch each day. Nanook would go over and knock Midget down and take her rubber "babies," and Midget wouldn't do anything about it. She would watch Nanook rip them up into tiny pieces and then, after Nanook was done, gather up the pieces and take them back to her dog bed.

One day Sam and I were playing fetch outside. I threw the ball, and Sam went and chased down the ball and brought it back to me. We did this for about fifteen minutes until I saw Midget watching us from behind the glass back door. I threw the ball and Samantha went to catch it and Midget just kept watching. It was like she was watching us with a face full of regret. Like she knew she had wasted so much time in her life being mean and tough and now for what? For her rubber "babies" all picked apart in pieces.

So Samantha and I threw the ball and we watched Midget watching us from the back door and looking so lonely. "Okay, Sam, that's enough," I said, and we gathered up our tennis balls.

I went back inside to Midget and she was surrounded by ripped-up pieces of her toys. She started to gather the tiny pieces back up again to and take them back to her bed. It was like she even had trouble finding them because of the blackness in her eyes. She was whining from the pain in her legs.

"Midget?" I said. "Did Nanook rip up another one of your toys?" I picked up the rubber pieces and I brought them back to Midget's bed. I gathered the pieces there and Midget lay down beside them. I kept lining up pieces of ripped "babies" in front of her and I wondered when Midget was going to bite me. But she didn't. I went over to Nanook, the giant white dog, and I ripped one of Midget's chew toys out of her mouth.

It was covered in slobber and disgusting. I put it back in Midget's bed and she sniffed it. Then I sat down beside her, and it was like she was saying, "I'm so full of regrets. I tried to be a big dog for so long, but I'm not. I'm just a little dog and I'm so afraid."

So I reached out and I pet Midget for the first time. I pet her coarse hair and I heard Nell say, "Oh gosh, Scott. You're the first person she's let pet her in years." Then Nell walked away, and I saw that Midget was my great-aunt Nell. It was years in the future and I was trying to tell her in the nursing home how much I loved her. I pet Midget slow and nervous and it was like we were finally friends. I laughed and said, "I can't believe she's letting me do this. I can't—" and then Midget whipped her head and bit the fuck out of my hand. I looked down at my hand and I felt myself shaking. The bite mark was bloody, but I didn't turn away.

I put out my hand and I tried to pet her again.

5.

Midget died a year later and no one cared except for Nell. My mom said, "I feel so much less nervous going to see Nell now that Midget is dead." In a letter that winter Nell told my mom that she was taking a senior citizens' ceramics class. She told my mom to send pictures of our cat Razy, who had just died, and she would make a ceramic version of him for Christmas. She told us she was making a ceramic version of Midget too.

But when we came to see her the next spring, we'd forgotten all about it. We hugged and Samantha and Nanook jumped, excited, on our legs. We talked about the drive down and our plans for the week. Nell told us how she wanted to take us to Colonial Williamsburg. I listened to Nell tell us what she was fixing for dinner and then I had to go pee. I walked down the hallway and I saw pictures of Midget on the wall. I saw pictures of my great-grandparents and all of the sudden I stopped, scared. I saw the ceramic Midget sitting in the corner. She was staring at me. The white was the perfect shade of white and the spots were the right amount of black. It was Midget come back to life.

I tried to breathe and I tried to walk but I was stopped still. I was seven years old again. The ceramic Midget growled and snapped and snarled, "Motherfucker, motherfucker." And so I ran. Just like right now, writing about Midget, I know she will reappear. She will jump right out of these words. She will materialize from these sentences and bite the motherfucker reading them. She is here now, and I am saying what she would say. "I'm not afraid of you—you reading fucks. You're afraid of me. Motherfucker. Motherfucker. I'm going to kill you all."

Pet Etymologies

Mark Leidner

Isis was a stray black kitten I found in the azaleas at around age ten or eleven—and the Egyptian goddess who resurrected the divine king Osiris. She is considered the mother of pharaohs and generally believed to assist the dead in entering the afterlife.

Buckwheat was an orange-and-tan mixed-breed rescue—and the only African American character on *Our Gang*, a series of comedic short films made in the thirties and forties that we watched growing up in the eighties. Because *Our Gang* featured Buckwheat playing as an equal with other white children, he was initially seen as a pioneering example of desegregation in an otherwise completely segregated mainstream entertainment landscape. By the fifties, however, Buckwheat had come to be seen as a racist caricature of African Americans.

Of none of this were we aware when we gave our Buckwheat

her name, and when Eddie Murphy recapitulated the stereotype on *Saturday Night Live*, we laughed without understanding.

Eddie—long black hair, perhaps part chow, perennially covered in dust and briars—walked out of the woods one day and decided to stay with us until he died. My dad named him after Eddie George, the then star running back of the Tennessee Oilers / Titans. Over the course of his eight seasons in the NFL, Eddie George amassed 10,441 rushing yards, 2,227 receiving yards, and 78 touchdowns. In 2016, Eddie George appeared on Broadway in *Chicago* as the hustling lawyer Billy Flynn.

Diego—a forty-five-pound black-and-tan part-kelpie rescue—is my "son." I became his "dad" when I married his "mother," who changed his name from Sundance. He'd been rescued from the streets of Dallas with a brother by a shelter who'd named them both Butch and Sundance. The names stopped having tandem meaning, however, when the brothers were adopted by separate families.

My spouse renamed Sundance Diego because Diego means James, which is her last name, and she thought it would be funny if her dog was named James James.

James the Greater was one of the twelve apostles of Christ and one of two apostles named James. He is considered the first apostle to have been martyred—but consensus ends there about who he was. According to one tradition, he spread Christianity in Iberia after the crucifixion. In tangent legend, he is labeled "Moor-killer," or Santiago Matamoros, for miraculously appearing to help an outnumbered Christian army defeat the emir of Córdoba eight hundred years after his death. Many traditions dispute, however, that James ever left Palestine at all. After he was beheaded in Jerusalem by King Herod Agrippa, the Roman vassal, James's followers supposedly moved his remains by stone boat to Galicia and buried them where the Cathedral of Santiago de Compostela would eventually stand—endpoint of The Way of St. James, the most renowned pilgrimage for medieval Christians.

Less is said about James the Lesser. The four times he is mentioned in the Gospels, it's just as a name in a list of apostles.

Years after Sundance became Diego, my wife saw a dog in Austin that looked just like him. She talked to the owner and found out he had once been named Butch and had come from the same Dallas shelter. Impressed by the serendipity of their meeting, they met up again a week later on the banks of a river outside of town and let the long-lost brothers play for an hour.

Butch was now Schnitzel.

Scout is a black mixed-breed—part border collie, part Lab—and the narrator in Harper Lee's *To Kill a Mockingbird*. Scout belongs to my sister-in-law, but my wife named her. In their hometown of Colusa, California, there is a community-wide reading program called the Virginia Yerxa (after the late school-board fixture and literacy advocate) Community Read, in which kids and adults all read and participate in events themed around a particular book. *To Kill a Mockingbird* was the book chosen the year that Scout was adopted, prompting my wife to suggest the name.

My late grandfather, a Louisiana Republican and farmer who raised my dad on a farm in south Texas, named his dogs after Democratic party politicians. I don't remember what the dogs looked like, but

I know they were mixed-breed rescues, and some of their names were Kitty (after Kitty Dukakis, author and wife of 1988 Democratic presidential nominee Michael Dukakis, former governor of Massachusetts and only the second Greek American governor in U.S. history after Spiro Agnew), Hillary (after Hillary Clinton), and Jesse (after Jesse Jackson).

Lady Susan is one of my sister's two extremely fluffy, dainty, petite white-and-gray cats—and the alluring and amoral protagonist in the eponymous novella by Jane Austen. Throughout *Lady Susan*, Lady Susan shamelessly manipulates and seduces single and married men alike in a quest for social advantage for herself and her daughter.

Lola is the other of my sister's extremely fluffy, dainty, petite white-and-gray cats—and the eponymous protagonist in *Lola Montès*, a 1955 French film by German-born director Max Ophüls based on the life of Lola Montez, the Irish dancer and courtesan. The film tells the story of the most famous of her many notorious affairs, including those with Franz Liszt, the Hungarian composer, and Ludwig I, the king of Bavaria until 1848, when he became the only German ruler to abdicate during the revolutions that swept what is now that country. The most expensive European film ever produced at the time, *Lola Montès* flopped at the box office but has also been said to have greatly influenced the French New Wave.

This is not really related to their names, but once, my wife and I were asked to cat-sit Lady Susan and Lola while my sister was traveling for work. Every day that we drove over to her house, we would find that Lady Susan had found the paper towels—in a closed cabinet, in the pantry—removed an entire roll, taken it into the kitchen, and then set the paper towel roll in the self-watering bowl, where it soaked up all the water in the reservoir and completely ruined the roll of paper towels. Three days in a row, we came to my sister's house to find that this had happened, despite having hidden the paper towels in different, increasingly more difficult-to-access cabinets. It seemed so unlikely that any cats, let alone a cat as dainty as Lady Susan, would be able to find the paper towels and do the same thing—removing, by the way, her ability to access her own water—three times in a row that it felt, upon entering my sister's house on the second and third day, as if we were entering a time-loop into yesterday or yesterday's yesterday.

Here is how my brother describes the naming of his and his wife Courtney's two cats, Pongo and Rocky:

> Before we even got cats, me and Courtney decided that Pongo was a great name for a spunky, playful, and charming cat. When we got the kitty that was to be Pongo, he fit the name so well it was like name at first sight. For Rocky, we were undecided for a while. Courtney wanted to name him Sebastian, but I knew one or two people named Sebastian and didn't want their memories confounding how I thought of the cat. We settled on Rocky, I think, due to his unusually clumsy movements and lazy postures. Rocky thinks he is a dog from time to time, so we'll call him "third dog," and so, working backward logically, we call Pongo "true cat."

Here is how Courtney describes the naming of her and my brother's two dogs, Liza and Yogi:

Yogi was found alone in the woods on a hike by Dan, my friend, whose nephew originally named him Rick—a name I didn't think fit. Yogi looked like a fluffy bear cub to me, so I wanted his new name to be bear-related. I also thought that Yogi Bear was an appropriate reference because Yogi was always getting into trouble, so I settled on Yogi. Liza's foster parents named her. Her mom always named the foster dogs after bonobo apes she worked with at Emory University. Apparently one was named Liza. Liza's name seemed to fit her fine, so I left it.

Liza likes to lick. She will often lick Yogi's eyes while he's trying to sleep—until he growls at her. When Diego goes over to visit Yogi, Liza, Rocky, and Pongo, Diego loves to play with Liza. He seems proud to be part of a big, rambunctious, poly-species pack. Unfortunately, he tends to corner Rocky and Pongo and have staring contests with them, inching closer and closer until either cat, hissing, swats him on the nose. Diego yelps and retreats, terrified, but five minutes later, he's staring them down in some new corner of the house. He's probably just perplexed by cats and wants to sniff them, but since they don't know that's all he wants, they won't let him near, and the tension increases until he gets swatted again. It's good for Diego to learn to respect other animals, though, so I'm glad Rocky and Pongo hold their ground.

Onomastikós is the Greek name for the origin, history, and use of proper names. My name is Mark, after my mother's brother. Whenever I looked up what "Mark" meant in the books that detail such things that one encounters as a kid, it always said my name meant "warlike"—from the Roman god Mars. At first I was disappointed because my name didn't mean something nice like "the chosen one" or "child of God" or "hope" like all the other names I wanted seemed to. One of my worst fears growing up (the other was dying in a house fire) was being drafted and sent to war. I wasn't "warlike" at all; I sometimes worried I was secretly warlike, though, in some way that hadn't yet manifested.

Eventually, however, perhaps because I had no choice, I found a way to be proud of "warlike." Sometimes wars were necessary, I rationalized, like the Civil War or World War II. Maybe it was cool to have a "dangerous" name. Then I grew up more and forgot about all this and stopped caring what my name meant. This period of not caring was probably the longest in my life. Recently, however, I came to a new plateau of real or fake enlightenment about names. I now believe (based on no research) that "Mark" is actually derived from the Latin *mare* which means "the sea," which is the same word "horse" and "Mary" (my mother's name) come from. The sea is where all creatures come from originally, so now to me my name means "from the sea."

I love how names exist in a ghostly space between private and public significance. There are things names mean that their havers aren't even aware of—significations of which others may only be aware, or about which the name-haver and name-sayer may disagree completely—as well as significations no one is aware of, yet which must still influence the name-haver's path through the world.

And how the history of a place and culture moves through its names without anyone but poets and scholars (and even them not very often) ever noticing.

And how much identity is like this—murky connotation cascading off our beings like the tail of a comet wherever we go and whatever we do without our direct perception of it or any of its effects.

An entire sea of context, often thousands of years of history or more, boiled down into a single droplet—sometimes a single syllable—with which people fix us as a substitute for all of that context.

And yet a name is also transparent—we often see through it, or forget it, or disregard it completely, or alter it, or consider ourselves or those who have it a redefinition of it, a stretching of its capacity rather than a fulfillment of its limitations.

An often-invisible historicity whistles around us, a radiation of identity—much of which we do not choose—but which to some extent we may choose to embrace or reject, to reinforce or reinvent—if only we can see what it is that these names say we are—like craning our necks to get a glimpse of our own auras, the auras some mediums claim to be able to see around our heads.

And also that this is true of every word—not just "names"—and is just as true of the obviously important words like "justice" and "love" and "person" as the seemingly unimportant ones like "of" and "and" and "the" and "with" and "out" that don't at first seem to name anything too terribly specific, but which actually name the most important things—relationships between other names for things—and whose expanded significations only begin to appear when they are removed from the flow of ordinary context.

SHELLS

Raegan Bird

In third grade my hamster was eaten alive by carnivorous bugs that hatched from the store-brand seed-and-nut blend that we fed him.

Chickens Are Real

Blake Butler

I thought I'd never have another pet. Since our family's miniature schnauzer died from diabetic fainting into a pool when I was nine, for which I blamed myself, I'd come to find pet owners pitiable, searching for something missing in a living body at last they could control. It's probably mirrored in my desire to never be close to anyone or anything again while watching my dad lose his mind to Alzheimer's.

*

It's not a coincidence that the house I first moved into with my future wife came with a coop in the backyard. A ramshackle structure, covered in shit, with little hearts cut in either side to allow air in. The previous owners had tried to change their mind last minute about leaving it behind. I'd found myself putting my foot down, illogically: *If you try to take the coop, we no longer want to buy the house*. I'm not sure what made me say it that way, or how they knew to acquiesce, though regarding my demand that the chickens remain part of the deal—something also promised, then retracted—the seller's agent reminded ours: "These are their pets."

Without the direct personal context regarding live fowl, I'd defaulted to the predominant belief that chickens aren't animals one keeps as friends. Somewhere within me, Werner Herzog's voice described their "bottomless stupidity, a fiendish stupidity"—a viewpoint that, coming out of a culture dependent on poultry as a staple, now seems to me to be willfully ignorant, unexamined. It mistakes the glare of even the most handsomely tufted fowl as incapable, rather than essentially unpandering, especially in comparison against the generously imagined depth of feeling of a dog, who eats its own waste.

*

But about *home*: Without the birds in our backyard, would the place from which we would begin to build the foundation of our marriage have had the same sense of somewhere *ours*? We already knew we weren't going to want children, and allergies and childhood fears held us back from the more usual forms of a mutual overseeing of other life. There wouldn't be a need to give a name to anything else living. I imagine we both thought we would be satisfied by making art, though if there's anything that doesn't need you, it's a sentence.

Our chickens didn't *need* us either. But we gave them names, and in return they made our household span beyond its walls, provided purpose not circumscribed to our imaginations. Here we were in the midst of possibility neither of us had realized we both needed.

*

Our starter birds, agreeably left behind from the flock of the homesellers as a gift, were a Polish hen named Watermane, with a head of tufted feathers like an explosion, and a Welsummer named Sheed (after Rasheed Wallace, my wife's hometown NBA hero). In the early days, we left them in the coop with the doors left wide open through the night. Obvious as it might seem now, no one warned us about what all might come in search of prey during sleep. One day not long after bedtime we heard the yard lurch full of what I can remember only now as *screaming*. By the time we made it through the yard, the whatever-it-was had slunk away into dark. There were blood and feathers all over everything, a kind of horror scene that might appear cartoonish until associated with real pain. Sheed's cold, blank stare seemed even more impenetrable then, unable to say what had happened, how it hurt, to ask us why we'd let it happen. It seemed as if she might even survive, well as she hid her wounds for days thereafter, until her body began rotting under her feathers.

Most chickens can't be expected to expire from old age, for obvious reasons. Yet there are the apparent differences that emerge in maturation when allowed—the slowed-down, motherly perspective older hens assume, watching the young ones wander around them as if waiting for their chance to let them know their place in the pecking order.

We wrapped the injured bird in a towel and lay her head down on a log to be lopped off. Sheed seemed to freeze and lie in wait as I held her still. My wife raised the hatchet and brought it down again through our pet's neck. The chicken's rigid body shook and spasmed for several moments in my hands, as go the rumors, before eventually she again went full limp. We buried her not far from where she'd slept, not knowing then that she'd be only one of several we would lose, each a lesson in caretaking for which the chickens paid with their lives.

*

From that point forward, Watermane, the Polish, started sleeping on the roof of the coop alone, perched as high and as far as she could get, or so I saw it, from the memory of her friend's demise. Maybe she just wanted to see the moon, to feel the breeze blow; more likely she wished that she could fly away. But to me she seemed so much sadder left alone, if still committed to her daily routines of consuming, laying, and sleeping.

Either way, that same sole-surviving bird would come to watch us in the kitchen through the window as we cooked. She would cock her head and study how I scrubbed the dishes, prepared coffee. For a couple years we still ate chicken meat bought from the store, its presence somehow disconnected in our minds from the animals we cared for, until one day it seemed too strange. Wasn't there something in the endless blank about their eyes—or was it a reflection of my own desires?

*

Dementia eroded my father's memory from the inside. He no longer remembered how to care for himself, much less another; he no longer could understand what was wrong or why or how to ask; he would fear things that didn't seem to others to be real. Though I try not to spend time thinking about it, I can feel that dark kernel passed along into my person, waiting to overtake me one day too. I will be relinquished in the same way, to the same unknowing; I will become meat again—mush.

In some ways, then, the greatest blessing you might ask for is to have your head cut off in one clean blow, by someone who will mourn you, even briefly; just like that.

*

After Sheed died, we bought a pair of black Orpingtons, Lindsey and Pyramid, from a farm guy off of Craigslist. We met him in a massive parking lot to fork over thirty bucks for two birds in a box. I can still remember how scared they seemed at first as we let them out, standing on the porch uncertain what might become of them. Though Pyramid would be snatched up by a hawk a few months later, Lindsey lived the longest of all the chickens we've yet had; a kind, reserved bird who often looked after the others like a mother, nervous but sweet.

Bing Bong and Crusher—the latter named after the Megadeth song that came on the radio as we drove back home from the chicken farm where we picked them out of several dozen silkies—remained inseparable until one got snatched up by the same hawk, who returned because the fence we'd raised around the coop still wasn't enough, each new death a minor lesson. Bing Bong was never the same alone—resigned to such timidity that we had to isolate her from the group so she could maintain access to feed, rarely interested even in eating, until in the end she hardly had the energy to stand. I used a broom handle to disconnect her head from her body.

Magic Johnson and Olex, bought from a breeder working out of a gas station in deep North Georgia, were perhaps our strangest pair. There was something different about Magic; how she walked more upright than other birds, how her hackle feathers made a mullet. Olex at once became my favorite bird for no clear reason other than premonition. She would sit still and sleep on my chest for as long as I'd allow. Shit luck turned that early favor into a death sentence: Olex made it hardly two weeks among the flock before I came out into the yard in time to see her being swooped up by a hawk, carried off to nowhere in a blink. *Bye, bird.* We decided to enclose the coop in heavy netting after that, creating a safe but impenetrable eyesore that would occupy our yard for the next year, with a gate the birds could come and go from under our supervision only.

We started locking the coop at night with padlocks, putting the birds away one by one like babies. Magic Johnson grew up enough to reveal that her odd demeanor was because she was actually a he—and thereafter began terrorizing the flock of ladies, insisting on mounting them as he patrolled the yard for their protection, even from my wife and me. That rooster would attack my legs whenever I tried to come

near, would fill the hours with his random crowing, even with the
training bowtie around his neck we bought in an attempt to mute
the noise. Local ordinance forbade such behavior in our neighborhood, and no one wanted him. We were forced to play the role of
executioner because the animal refused to play along with human
law. We came for him in the night, when he'd be sleepy, unaware.

Olex 2 and Snacky came from a farm in the midst of breakup.
The woman selling off her flock seemed downtrodden as we stood
amid her soon-to-be ex-boyfriend's land and picked two birds out
of the dozens she'd been assembling for years. Neither of these
birds ever seemed quite to fit in with the rest of ours, though; they
remained estranged, the closest version of the Herzogian animal as
described. The difference, as I saw it, was that these birds had not
been hand-raised. By having only a few around at a time, giving
them individual attention and space to graze, our prior chickens
were distinguished from these raised in relative captivity.

In the end, we learned that silkies were the breed for us. They have
blue ears and black skin, five toes on each foot; their feathers look
like hair; they look like little Muppets come alive, and are known
for friendliness and like to be petted. We ordered three of them,
along with another Polish to replace Watermane when at last she
got too old to see the hawks coming on her own. They arrived
through the mail in a box, each bird the size of a golf ball, not yet
two days old. We tore down our massive netted bird-complex and
replaced it with a much smaller, handmade wooden house, where
Woosh, $5 Bill, Anne Carson, and Hector hang out together, wait-
ing each day for us to come out and stand beside them and let them

chase bugs and bathe in dirt. It took a couple years of irregular heartache, but now we have a little family.

*

Watch a timid hen with depth perception issues, like our Hector, try to figure out each morning the least scary way to come down the walkway into the run. Find the same bird standing at the far end of the run just before a thunderstorm, staring out across the yard as if contemplating the passing day. See how Woosh will stand up for Hector against the other birds picking at her, as their biology commands; see how the pair sleep snuggled side by side in their box each night, how they stay near each other even in day; how they are, most obviously, *friends*.

Or how about the birds' undeniable excitement at being allowed out each morning, into the dawn? How most birds don't want to be picked up because they have work to do, or so they believe, and yet how obvious their satisfaction is in being bathed under warm water in the sink, then wrapped in a towel, their eyes rolled back in their head in pleasure, nearly even purring when petted the right way.

Or, then, the tricky sadness of going broody, wanting to spend all day in the laying box warming an egg, hoping to birth a child that never comes; how you can only break them of it with time and cool air; how it happens over and again. How you can take them out of their box and they will run right back to where they were and continue sitting haunched without proper food or water, whether or not the unfertilized egg is still underneath them.

What I see in a hen's face at moments like these is her modest heart laid bare. I have felt that hens are as much motivated by a desire to consume and lay as by their ongoing awareness of becoming prey, unabashedly alive behind their bulging, darting eyes.

*

What would a chicken do if it had hands? What language is there in their chirping, clucking; in how they bunch together, side by side? What might they know that we will never? It's an animal's greatest gift, perhaps, that we can't ask. Then what else might we demand of them?

Still, the meat of bird fills our plates. We've been taught to live with murder so many other ways, why sacrifice convenience, after all? Isn't this the way it's meant to be? Without some practice by which we allow our species to assert dominance over all else, how else could we survive our own egos?

If there's any justice, when at last the human race finally obliterates itself by way of the same ambient brutality we've come to accept as *how it is*, the birds won't remember us at all.

In the meantime, these birds, these tiny dinosaurs, provide us with relief: something to get up for, to come home to. I go out in the yard alone to tell them my problems or talk about the coming rain while I feed them cheese. I see my wife through the window in the yard talking to the birds in a voice I can't hear, leading them to half-flap half-fly across the yard in a small rush, and I go to join them.

Assignments

Yuka Igarashi

My kindergarten teacher was named Mrs. Berg. She used to sit in front of the class holding a mirror to her face, applying circles of lipstick to her cheeks and then rubbing them into her skin. During naptime, she would play a recording of Simon and Garfunkel's "Bridge Over Troubled Water." From her I learned the word "magnificent," was complimented on my dexterity with a yo-yo, and received a snail, which I brought home and named Emily. This was in Manhattan in the eighties. I liked Mrs. Berg very much.

Emily lived in a plastic takeout container. I liked to put lettuce in the container with her and watch her approach it. She advanced toward it, rotating her four tentacles around, and then attached the bottom of her head to it. The lettuce disappeared quickly into her body through her mouth, a suctioning hole surrounded by teeth. She seemed to eat a lot for her size. If given a watermelon rind, Emily climbed onto it and stayed there for days, until there was no red left. She was greedy and thorough, and this made her seem happy and smart to me. When I picked her up and put her on my arm, she didn't go into her shell. She kept moving forward, convincing me that she had a destination.

Among the personality traits I've assigned to Emily are "intrepid," "decisive," "strong-willed," and "resilient." After the school year ended, my family went on a trip to Japan and left Emily with a friend, who dropped her onto kitchen tile, cracked her shell, and flushed her down the toilet.

I remember I cried and my mom laughed at me, not without affection. Her laugh did not not comfort me. It said: Child, you have no idea what's coming. She must have been a little sad too. She was the one who was home most of the time with Emily, feeding and cleaning her.

In the apartment where we all lived, I once saw my dad bash my mom's head against the front door. My mom had just flicked a cigarette butt at him, or maybe called him a name. I remember thinking that whatever she'd done or said was mean. But so was the head-bashing. I remember my older brother standing in the doorway of our bedroom, looking at them, laughing at first because he thought they were playing. Then he was crying. I remember standing behind him, hiding.

I have seen, throughout my life, that animals want to be around my mom. She attracts them. After we left the city and moved to the suburbs, we owned three cockatiels. We "adopted" the next-door neighbor's cat—an obese, unfriendly, unneutered orange tabby that my mom renamed Tama, which means "ball" in Japanese, after his balls. Tama loved chicken wings. My mom baked them in the oven and Tama sat in her lap at the dining room table, eating out of her hands, growling and swiping his claws at her and at the wings. The way my mom was with all our pets was the way I wanted her to be with me. She paid attention to what they liked, and gave it to them.

I don't remember my classmates' snails, though my classmates must have had them. In my memory, during the kindergarten snail unit, we each got one snail, memorized snail facts, drew snails, and were taught to crochet spiral patterns, to better appreciate snail shells. But in my memory, only my snail survived past the end of the unit, and only I spent the following years writing stories in which the main character was a snail.

I still like telling people about Emily. Sometimes I will think about snails, in general—their slowness, the way they hide, their attachment to their houses, the murky residue they leave behind—and feel calmer, safe, anchored.

When we moved to the suburbs, Mrs. Berg wrote me a letter that said the teachers and students at my new school would be surprised that a "smart kid" had come from the city. I remember feeling pleased, happily attaching these words to my idea about myself. I didn't think about why anyone would be surprised, or if anyone was. I understand now that Mrs. Berg hadn't thought about it either. Most people are just saying things.

What am I trying to say when I say I used to have a snail who, under my care but actually under my mom's care, lived for an unusually long time? I think it's supposed to say: I had an acceptable childhood. It's supposed to say: I have never needed much. It's supposed to say: Give me something small and temporary and I will make it big and permanent. I will hold onto it. But these all seem like sentimental lies to me. Like really what I'm trying to do is to make sure you don't know me.

Love

Sarah Manguso

Her death speeds toward us from the future. We're starting to run toward it now. I'm holding all six pounds of her, purring and stinking, and I'm speed-walking so as not to jostle her. She doesn't make a sound.

I bring special food home, but she doesn't eat it.

I research euthanasia, feeling helpless. Then I brush her all over while she sits on the windowsill and purrs. Bring her into the bathroom and run the hot shower. She lies in my lap and breathes. Then I hand-feed her the liquid salmon and she eats it. She just needs to keep her head elevated in order to swallow! Rig up some elevated dishes. Give her another steam bath.

She eats a little more of the wet food in the night, but nothing the next day. Give her a twenty-minute steam bath. She isn't quacking while she inhales anymore. Then she starts quacking again.

A. takes her to the hospital at midnight. They come home at three thirty, and she's meowing her head off. Her nose has been suctioned and she's spent some time in an oxygen tent. She drinks some water and seems much improved. Earlier in the day we'd discussed euthanizing her.

The next day, I need to syringe-feed her. She can't smell the food, but once it's in her mouth she seems to like it. How long will I do this for her?

She won't eat or drink or groom, and she's too tired to finish her bowel movement; it hangs off her and falls off somewhere in the kitchen or in our bed. She smells bad. I'm not sure she can even sleep; she seems half in and half out of her body.

Schedule her death for five o'clock tomorrow afternoon. My birthday.

She crawls onto my neck at four in the morning, burrows under the covers, onto my chest, as if trying to get into me.

Cats are supposed to hide when they die, but ours wanted to burrow into our bodies. Wants to.

My good, beautiful kitty, small warm weight on my lap on this last day.

The doctor takes her away to place a line in her foot. Then he brings her back and we hold her and tell her how much we love her. I sing her "I Love My Kitty" one last time. Then we invite the doctor back in, and he gives her a shot through her line. It takes about three seconds. Her head drops into the crook of my arm, her chin resting on my right hip.

My cursory scientific knowledge doesn't explain what I sense, which is the exiting of an anima, a word I've never used before, never needed. When her body goes limp, I sense that something has disappeared. What is it and where has it gone? Words I have assiduously avoided until now. *Life force, soul.* The grand total of the body's biophysical processes.

Then she receives a second shot that stops her heart. It takes about two seconds. The doctor listens for her heartbeat and declares she's gone. I look into her face, her head drooped, her eyelids drooped, her eyes still wet—and then we go home.

I feel as if something is wringing me out, binding me in a cast so tight that I can't take a deep breath. I fear I didn't love her enough, at the very end. I don't know what she was thinking when she died on my lap. I don't know anything she ever thought. It is more than I can bear.

The creature sensed and judged and moved and breathed. It lived, and now it does not live. What has changed? Something that once moved is now still; her body was warm and is now cold. The energy that animated her body dissipated and joined the rest of the universe, spread out into a greater volume, the energy that for seven or eight years was once concentrated in an area the size and shape of a small cat.

Every posture I took in the house for eight years was in expectation of her on my chest or lap or under my bent knees. My body is still ready for her.

I watch videos of her playing. It makes me feel better, remembering all the fun she had.

Take the lint brush to my desk chair, where she took so many naps. But then I see a smear or a bit of fluff somewhere else. I want to vomit. The bits of old sneeze and pawprints crush me. The fact of her body. I spoke to her and sang her her own special songs. She cannot hear me anymore.

The house is empty, quiet, and clean.

I keep returning to the moment I surrendered her.

I try to think that she had absorbed all possible love, that she was unable to take in any more, that this inability to absorb any further love was not incidental to her death but equivalent to it.

I will have to learn to love her beyond the fact of her body.

It is comforting to watch documentaries about people who do extraordinary things. People who do extraordinary things are as absolutely alone as I am.

Today, I will not get back into bed until nighttime.

My god, my little friend is gone.

In the last days of her life, she sought a kind of closeness she had never previously needed. To be right on top of me. *Skin to skin*, they tell you after you give birth. Skin-to-skin contact keeps the baby healthy because it was so recently part of the mother's biophysical system. Toward the end, the cat seemed to need such a system. She was expressing her imminent reabsorption into the universe, energy seeping into the air, as a body being absorbed into another body. She was expressing that unavoidable state, which was barrelling toward us, as an act of love.

And it worked; on some level she had convinced me of her metaphor, for the first two days without her I felt as if something had been torn out of my body.

I skim books about how to speed through grief, to anticipate and pounce on each stage of it, to express it and excrete it through therapy, to neutralize it, deodorize it, clean it up—it's all the same. Then I find the following sentence: *The grief that you are feeling now is perfect.*

Since her final illness, a respiratory blockage that was probably cancer metastasized from her intestines, she had been leaving her urine in the corner of her litter box, uncovered—her usual indication that she was unwell. That last little wet circle, no bigger than a silver dollar, demented me when I saw it again after we returned, bereft, with her empty blue carrier. I wanted to scoop up the lump of clay and save it in a plastic bag. I wanted to massage it, to sniff it, to eat it. My husband threw away that last box of litter, that last circle that marked the evidence of her life and her place in the world.

What did we call her? *Toast*, for she looked like a golden-brown slice of it, but more often I addressed her as *Kittykins* or *Lady Meowington* or *Softy*.

For the last few months, whenever I saw her, it was hard not to blurt *Hi, beautiful.*

Baby, my baby. I'd become one of those people who call an animal *Baby*, even though I have a child, too, two years younger than the cat. I told my son that the cat was special because she was the first creature I ever took care of, and that taking care of her had made me want to take care of other creatures, and that she is the reason I decided to become pregnant and give birth to him. That without her he wouldn't have existed. I told him this when he was five years old. *Without the kitty I wouldn't be alive*, he carefully said.

One month after she dies, we have houseguests. On the way home from school, I ask my son, *Guess who's waiting at home for us. — Dad? —No.* He thinks for a moment. *—The kitty?*

At the top of the concordance of my spoken words over the last eight years would be the phrase *Good girl*. I said it in my kitty voice, a silly mess of deranged vowels and explosive enthusiasm. I said it to the kitty when she caught her string on a jump or when she pounced and clapped her front paws around the furniture leg. She always loved watching a long string slowly moving around a fixed post. She especially loved it when a string was pulled very slowly underneath a pile of lightly crumpled newspaper. The scent of fresh newspapers delighted her. She rolled in them sensually.

Good girl, I'd croon when she cuddled in my lap, curling into a loaf. If I petted her she'd invert her head and show her white muzzle and chin.

Her orange tummy always came as a bit of a shock, like the bright orange pubic hair of a long-ago blond boyfriend. The first time I saw it I must have shown my surprise, because he immediately said, *I know.*

Now her bits of undercoat are the badge of my grief. I don't roll them off with the lint brush anymore. Someday they will all be gone.

There is no place where she is, anymore. The cat *isn't*. But the clay tablet with her pawprint pressed into it, the lock of fur, the box of ash, those are things that *are*, and that remind or even prove that she also was, once.

The literal necessity of the gravestone.

I don't want to look inside my son's play tent in the corner of his room. There must still be some claw tips inside, long ago shed. I don't want to know how much of her body is there. It is so terribly easy to picture her black-lined green eyes, so expressive, looking up at me—*How have you left me here, forgotten about me, for so many days?*

In the last year of her life, she liked to watch movies. Amateur videographers, angels living against nature's frontier, would leave piles of birdseed outdoors, under trees, and set up cameras to capture the birds and squirrels that came. And the kitty would watch the footage as closely as any human person ever watched a favorite show.

The kitten first came to my husband one afternoon, more than seven years ago, while he was working in the garage. She meowed loudly, and we gave her some water and tuna in ramekins on the front steps of the house. On the second or third day we left notes on the neighbors' doors. *Have you lost a kitten?* But no one had lost her.

Then we lost her. A day or two later, we heard tiny meows coming from the canopy of the avocado tree that hung over the property. My husband nailed together some two-by-fours end to end and stapled a cardboard box to the top. We put some water and tuna in the box. A few days later the kitten climbed down.

My husband brought a cardboard carrier home from the pet store and intimated that it might be difficult getting her into the box, but I knew it would be easy. I'd already picked her up several times. *Watch!* I picked her up and put her in the box. Before I could close the lid, she jumped out, and I learned something about cats.

Domani

Ann Beattie

I once complained to my friend Harry Mathews about having to leave Key West, where he and his wife and my husband and I were living, to teach for the semester in Virginia. It was January, very pleasant in Florida. Feeling sorry for myself, I added that where I was going, I'd have no pets, not even a houseplant. (We were flying; other times, my husband has to drive in a car jungle of exotic plants.)

A huge box arrived at our house in Virginia a week later. I did not approach the box, which in any case I could not have lifted. Husband, at end of day: "What is that box on the front porch?" Wife: "I assumed it was art supplies you'd ordered." Inside, from Hammacher Schlemmer, a large stuffed toy dog, approximating a black Lab. For no good reason—though I consider its name perfect—my husband named it Domani. Had we wanted to mail our refrigerator somewhere, we had the perfect packaging. My husband really had to do some fancy stomping to prepare the box for recycling.

I began to put Domani in pictures I sent Harry, without comment: the dog under the newly blooming lilacs; Domani seen from behind, looking out the front door; Domani's head stroked by a visitor (art shot: close-up of fingers wiggling over dog's ear); Domani in bed, his head turned attentively toward me, when I had a fever of 102.

I know (though I never watched the show) that a standing joke on *Scrubs* was that a similar dog popped up here and there around the characters' house. I didn't intend to scare our plumber, as he turned on the overhead light in the dark downstairs bathroom to find himself standing knee-to-nose with Domani.

The dog's tail is the least realistic part: a bit too wide, too long—a real Princess Di's bridal train of a tail. The paws don't look exactly like actual paws, though the designer carefully considered standing dogs and did a credible job of permanent paw placement. Domani's head is turned slightly, as if he hears distant music, or is about to move. He's a little sway-backed now, as a couple of children have jumped on Horsie.

Why don't we have a "real" dog? Our answer is usually that we "travel too much," that "we're too busy and Ann would be the one stuck with taking care of it ha ha," or that we're both allergic to dogs. There are certainly those who wonder about our immature sense of humor.

Unlike the plants, given away (*"All my pretty ones. Did you say all?"*) those times they aren't jungled on the back seat, Domani was removed from Virginia when I finished teaching and remains in Maine. His initial transportation was probably his first and last car ride. We return to him in May, as we do to spring's lilacs, to dried-up ink cartridges in my printer.

This year when we got back, I was in No Mood to greet Domani. My best friend of fifty years had died in San Francisco. I looked bleakly at our garden springing up, expressed no interest when my husband began hanging suet for the birds. Once I put Domani on the sofa, placing his nose close to the window, but only because I was vacuuming. I didn't look out to see what he saw. It seemed like all jokes were over.

After my best friend died, a woman who'd known my best friend's dog since he was a puppy stepped forward to adopt him. No good deed goes unpunished: the dog bit her employee and was exiled to Doggie Boot Camp for training. After the memorial service the dog returned to the woman's apartment, and my best friend's sister went with her daughter to meet him. This encounter would be a sort of post-death bonding with her brother. The dog bit her leg. Then the dog bit her daughter.

Following the account I've just given, another friend out west emailed me: I should adopt the dog. She didn't exactly say that the dog was sending me a message, but that's what I extrapolated from her email. I never doubted that she was serious.

Further background: I used to be afraid of dogs. My mother was raised with dogs that frightened her (and every woman in the house, apparently), so if we were outside and a dog approached—leashed, or not—we crossed the street or, when I was small enough, she picked me up. It took me over twenty years to realize that I loved dogs. They were everywhere in the seventies. Hippies had dogs. Therefore, if I wanted to have friends, I'd better get over my fear of dogs. I pretty much did, and exhibited the zeal of the convert. I lived in a house where there were two dogs, then three; later, dog #3 became "my" dog. Flip forward in time: some friends in Maine happily let my husband and me take care of Sandy, their golden retriever, every summer when they went with their kids on wonderful dog-free vacations. We would put Sandy in the convertible and take him for ice cream. We moistened his dry dog food with bacon grease. When his owners returned and called to arrange a time to get him, we listened with desperation to the incoming message and did not pick up the phone. Some people who visited simply thought he was our dog. He was not. He died about six years ago, though photos of him remain in our house. I once had an author's photo taken with him. I thought his owners would be amused, but all they did was smile and nod when they saw it.

I'm writing this in Maine, after being asked to contribute to this anthology. I just went downstairs and looked at Domani, in a camouflage hat my husband sometimes wears while painting outdoors. It looks slightly better on the dog, but it's the sort of hat that anyone who wears it is going to have to live down. I didn't plunk the hat on his head. Must have been the dinner guests. Well, Domani's had a wolf puppet crouched on his back before, and he's worn a tiara. He's a magnet for the ridiculous.

I do notice that even in the absence of evidence, I've assumed Domani is a male. Well, I live with my husband. Harry, and my friend in San Francisco, and his dog, and the late, great Sandy were all males, so why not assume the likelihood of masculinity? But now that I think of it, my husband gave Domani an androgynous name. Subconsciously, all these years, I've assumed I was having my way with a male: Let's see you in profile, as you gaze out the window! Stand near the lilacs: you can do it, just for a second, back up, you don't need to take off your hat, do you have to tie your shoelace right this second, do you see that dark raincloud racing across the sky, could you just … ? Have *you* ever tried to get a man to stand where you want him to stand in a photograph? They're always fleeing, as if they're self-igniting firecrackers that had better get out of their own way before the explosion.

Of course, sometimes they just slip away. My best friend simply didn't show up for work one day. Lives happen whatever way they do, no matter how speakers at memorial services try to make sense of things. Being in control is an illusion.

You want to know the fate of my best friend's flipped-out dog. I don't know it. Okay, second best, at least a quasi-happy ending? Did I feel a rekindling of affection for Domani? How about a little projection, since we all know writers are devoted to that? Some personification, at the very least? Such as: I'm walking through the house and there's Domani, just as I left him (with the addition of the hat plunked on his head). What would a dog think, positioned, as he is, so that the chair's monotonously repeated fabric pattern would be all he could see—unable, as he is, to move his head? Well, he'd be bored, that's what. To alleviate the tedium, he might silently hum a tune (the closing song at my friend's memorial service was a very nice rendition of "I'll Be Seeing You"), or he might conjure up Pinocchio, who wanted to be "a real boy," or he might do what so many of us do when we're at a loss, and think up a joke. I don't think it would be about the trauma of the box he was shipped in, and since he never met his benefactor, his joke couldn't be about Harry. He'd want to be politically correct, of course. Being a modest fellow, he'd already know he couldn't compete with the acerbic wit of Trevor Noah. But he might turn his head just a little more, and focus his gaze, with his perfectly placed, amber-colored plastic eyes, on me: *There's Ann*, he'd think, *imagining things, yet again.* "Woman walks into a bar," he'd begin.

GRACE HAIKUS

Mallory Whitten

when she eats yogurt
she holds the container with
her paws, face submerged

she likes to chase light
and reflections around, she
doesn't understand

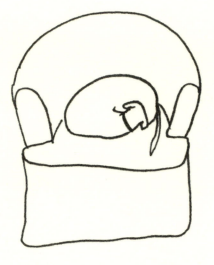

she went through a phase
where she licked her butthole for
a lot of the day

she's been my friend for
five years and she has never
said a word to me

ME AND DUCHENE

Sam Pink

Yeah, there we were.

Me and Duchene.

Do, fuckin, shane.

See, me and Duchene, we were like a team.

Partners.

When it was just me and Duchene, man, the whole world could burn.

As long as me and Duchene were together, it didn't matter.

Nothing mattered as long as it was me and Duchene.

*

Duchene was nine weeks old.

A black Labrador puppy.

Big glassy eyes and rolls of shiny fur hanging off his face and body.

Ears from here to the moon and teeth like little swords.

Fuckin Duchene ...

"You gotta lotta nerve, Duchene!" I said, slapping his legs out from beneath him, in my brother's basement.

My brother and his wife were gone for a couple weeks and I was house/Duchene-sitting.

It was the week of Christmas.

Just me and Duchene.

*

When it was me and Duchene, man, the whole world was a cake and we were just frosting hounds.

"Ow, fuck," I said, as he jumped up and bit my beard.

I was on my hands and knees, alternating between wrestling with him and looking out the window at the slow-falling snow.

The backyard shone bright white, expansive, leading all the way back to a couple sheds full of firewood.

We wrestled on the cold tile floor.

Fuckin Duchene.

His paws and forearms were already very large.

He kept hopping in and out, sometimes falling when his paws slid out from under him.

That's Duchene ... always trying to get somewhere but the world ends up moving under his feet.

"You stink, man," I said, as he tugged at my sweatshirt sleeve, ass in the air and half moons under his eyes.

He had huge floppy ears, the undersides of which smelled almost exactly like prosciutto.

Ol Sciutts Duchene ...

He bit me too hard again.

"Hey," I yelled.

Then I chest-bumped him while growling and barking.

He looked shocked, ears back, eyes wide when I barked.

He sat back, lifting his paw a little, falling over.

"Don't fuck with me, Duchene, you're not gonna like how it goes. We're partners, goddamnit."

He lay on his back, paws at chest, ears strewn across the floor letting rise the light smell of prosciutto.

"Fight me!" I growled.

Then I howled.

He scurried up and came at me again.

The howling always set him off.

When I barked, Duchene listened, but when I howled, man oh man.

Fuckin Duchene ...

Short-fuse temper.

You bring the flame, better believe Duchene will bring the boom.

I grabbed his leg and tripped him, then lifted his ear and took a huge-ass rip.

SNNNNNNIIIIIFFFFFFFFFF!!!!

Falling back onto the tile, I lay on my back kicking my legs and yelling, "Hoooooooooooooooooo."

Because all things considered, Duchene had that good shit.

I lifted his ear and rubbed it on the outer webbing between my thumb and pointer finger.

Took a big hit.

SNIFF!

I dropped the ear and reeled backward, yelling, "Hooooooooooo."

Duchene wagged his tail.

His tail was still so small and worm-like, skinny.

He had boogers in the corners of his eyes.

"You better getcher act togedder, Duchene," I said, pointing at him.

He jumped up and bit my finger, vaguely suckled it.

But man, I mean, that's just Duchene.

All guts and ears.

All play, all war.

A real son of a bitch.

Fuckin Duchene.

*

I learned after a couple days that the only way to calm him down
so I could get anything done, or try to catch up on sleep, was to
run him around for at least an hour or two at some point early in
the day.

I would wake up at like f to his whining, let him out of his locked
prosciutto cavern, and he would display what can only be described
as loose-cannon energy.

A rogue agent.

A real motherfucker, that one.

Cuz Duchene, see, he was nobody's bitch.

Duchene had a heart of gold, sure, but that gold burst forth in
terrible geysers.

Liquid.

It boiled and spat.

Scalding.

So I'd take him out into the backyard.

Standing there in the growing dawn, last of my morning boner dying in my sweatpants, holding a cup of steaming coffee as Duchene ran around, eating acorns and sticks and pissing on things.

I'd throw a tennis ball around, bounce it, throw it off the shed.

He was becoming more and more sure on his feet every day.

Sticks were his favorite.

He loved sticks.

One thing about Duchene, you pick up a stick and drag it along the ground, he's coming for it.

Bet your sweet ass Duchene's gonna tail you for that stick.

It's already his, baby.

"Come on!" I yelled, hitting the stick against the ground, running him up the rocky side hill, through a big pile of leaves.

His run was funny.

Looked kind of snake-like, sidewinding, the way his legs never really left the ground, just rocked back and forth, ears flopping up and down in perfect time with it.

Stunning, really.

Fuckin Duchene.

We ran up and down the rocky incline again and again.

"Good boyyyyy," I said.

I stopped in the yard and planted the stick, holding the other end.

Duchene jumped at it, biting and tugging.

He growled a comically high-pitched growl.

I tripped him with the stick.

"You fucking dork."

He fell face-first and rolled, and got up, growling.

I ran around and he chased me.

I had to stop repeatedly to remove acorns or rocks from his mouth.

A light snow/sleet began to fall.

It wasn't that cold, though.

So very nice.

Fall's colors covered up by white.

There were skinny trees along the forest between my brother's house and the neighbor's.

The snow-covered trees shook, possessing an ominous energy.

I dragged the stick down the hill and over the wooden walkway, back to the patio.

"Come on, Duchene."

We went inside.

He humped a blanket on the tile for a few strokes, then pawed it out like pizza dough, laid on it.

I did a gratuitous slicking-back motion on his shiny little head as he licked his lips and got red droopy eyes.

I learned over the next couple days, as we developed our routine, that this was standard.

He'd be running all over, biting everything, growling, wagging his tail and hopping around, then suddenly stop, lie down, and his face would age thirty years instantly, sagging and red-eyed with these weird other eyelids covering the bottom half of his open eyes.

After that, it was only moments before he fell asleep for a couple hours.

Lifting his head in still-asleep confusion, focused on nothing, licking his lips a few last lazy times, tongue barely coming out by the end.

Chlup chlup … chhhh …

Fuckin Duchene.

I got myself a glass of water and looked out the back door at the yard, at the snow accumulating slowly.

Something about it looked threatening.

Like it hid some unforeseen harm.

"We must always be vigilant, Duchene," I said loudly and sternly, my hands behind my back.

He sighed deeply, licked his lips.

Long as it was me and Duchene, though, it didn't matter.

They could all come for us.

We'd be right here.

*

In a nearby basement, a dimly flickering light taps in a dark room.

Various jars of formaldehyde, vials, blood-stained tools, anatomical diagrams.

The sound of dripping, heavy breathing.

As things come into focus, a man sits on a throne of dog skulls.

He wears a long cloak with puppy-skull shoulder blades.

He stares blankly.

Cages all around him.

He raises an oxygen mask to his emotionless face with blood-covered hands.

He inhales deeply, closing his eyes in ecstasy, opens them, pupils dilated, animal-like, ringed.

The oxygen mask falls to the ground.

We follow a tube from the mask along the grimy ground, past chewed-up toys, blankets, water bowls.

The tube leads into a cage holding numerous puppies, muzzles taped shut, eyes panicked, more tubes just under their ears.

The man inhales deeply, groans.

Melts into his throne.

UNNHHHHHH.

He reaches to the side, groping around on a lab tray, until he finds a pile of thin, fuzzy, floppy objects.

Crumbly black scabs along the edges.

He raises one to his face and sniffs devilishly, then rubs it all over his face, eyes closed.

"Guhhhh," he groans, biting his lip, nostrils flared.

His ecstasy is disrupted by a door opening, light from outside spilling in, some snowflakes.

A henchman drags in a squirming sack.

He opens the sack onto the ground, and puppies hop around, biting each other's ears.

"Here you go, boss," he says. "You want me to, ah, getcha anything else?"

"Yesssss," whispers the man on the throne, as he touches a small television playing surveillance footage.

The footage shows a man and a small black dog running around a snowy backyard, playing with sticks.

As he stares at the TV, in a trance, we slowly zoom in on his eyes, reflecting the puppy hopping around and chasing the man with a stick.

A quiet "You gotta lotta nerve, Duchene!" can be heard through the TV's tiny speaker.

"Duchene," whispers the man on the throne.

*

"You gotta lotta nerve, Duchene!" I said.

I was microwaving a mug full of water and dry dog food.

He was hopping around, ears flopping.

"You better getcher act togedder, or the chief is gonna filet our asses good!"

I hadn't really slept in a week and a half but our mornings were always fun.

Both of us delirious in the cold dawn.

He'd come to understand the significance of me opening the microwave door and beeping the buttons.

See Duchene, Duchene's always been a smart boy, you see.

Guy like Duchene always has the scoop of whatever biz.

A real wiseguy.

A real cutie pie.

He'd be hopping around with his ears flopping before I'd even hit "start" on that microwave, man.

Yeah, Duchene always knew the score.

Fuckin Duchene.

After he ate I took him out and ran him around for ten minutes so he could take a shit.

He picked up sticks and carried them around until he found a replacement.

Clasping a large stick in his mouth sideways, he shit a steaming pile.

"Come on, buddy, let's go," I said, clapping and walking back toward the house.

I had to put him back in his prosciutto den.

I'd been invited to go shooting at an outdoor range.

The guy who owned the local gun store and I had become friends.

*

The range was down a long dirt road, back in the woods.

It was cold, gray, and rainy.

"There he is," said the old man, as I opened the fence and came in.

Nobody else was there.

There was a rifle range, a trap range, and a pistol range, with steel targets.

He sat on a chair, benchresting a bolt-action rifle.

He pulled the bolt back and a casing flipped out.

I set down my plastic carrying case and got out my pistol.

"Why don't you take a couple from back here at fifty yards and see what you can do," he said.

I began loading a magazine.

He told me about jackrolling someone.

Usually when we hung out he told me very long stories about his work in the Marines and law enforcement.

He told me there was 0.05 percent of the population that would just always be criminal.

He pushed the bolt forward on his empty rifle.

Jackrolling, he explained, involved using a pocketknife to kill someone in seconds.

"Kkkkkkkkk," he said, pointing to his neck, then his leg, "you gettem here, or down here, they're gone in seconds."

I put my magazine into the pistol and racked the slide and took some shots at a target fifty yards away.

BOP … BOP … BOP BOP … BOP.

When we went to look, I'd put four in the target, mostly to the left.

The old man said not bad, but I was pulling them left.

He had me show him my hold and stance.

"There's the problem," he said, right away.

I was pinning my right-hand thumb beneath my left-hand thumb and pulling left when I shot.

We went over to a thirty-yard range, with steel plate targets in various formations.

"Practice over here, and make sure to practice some draws too," said the old man, then he went to the clubhouse to warm up.

A combination of snow and rain began to fall.

Ground all mud.

My fingers, nose, and cheeks wet and numb.

I loaded a couple magazines.

I put a magazine in my coat pocket and put one into the pistol.

Thumbed the slide lock.

Shik.

Held the pistol against my solar plexus with both hands, my finger off the trigger.

I took a breath and let it out slow.

I lifted the pistol, sighted, and took a shot at a tree of steel targets, designed to swing around to the other side if hit with a power-ful-enough round.

Using the new grip.

Ting.

The bullet hit the steel target and it swung around.

I went up the tree, hitting all eight, missing only once.

The new stance seemed very secure.

I shot the last two rounds on a single swinging steel plate, about twenty yards away.

The case flipped outward, and the slide locked back, smoke exiting the chamber.

I laughed.

Wow.

I brought the pistol back to my solar plexus and ran over to another target, probably twenty yards away from where I stood.

The target was meant to simulate a person holding another person hostage, with a plate just off to the side of where the hostage's head would be.

I extended the pistol and shot, *ting*, hit the hostage-taker's head.

I shot again, *ting*.

I went through a couple more magazines.

The woods around me cold and damp, sky slush-gray and leaky.

My face and fingers losing feeling.

The old man walked back over, hands in his coat pockets.

He watched me shoot a magazine.

I hit everything I shot at, swinging targets back and forth on the tree.

"A-*ha*!" he said.

"Holy shit, man, you were right," I said.

"Sometimes a little coaching doesn't hurt," he said, hands in his pockets and nodding.

*

Back at home, I put some music on and stripped the pistol while Duchene took a nap.

I sprayed oil all over the inside of the frame and the entire slide and barrel.

Cleaned out all the buildup and applied lube.

Duchene breathed oinkily, his chin extended and on my balled-up coat.

He began snoring.

Fuckin Duchene.

Sleeping on the job.

I put the pistol back together and racked the side a couple times.

Pointed it toward the ground, looked down the sights, holding it steady, all three posts aligned, pulled the trigger, *click*, held it pressed, racked the slide, slowly let the trigger go, felt the reset *tuk*, and pulled the trigger again, *click*.

Good to go.

"ONE MUST AT ALL TIMES MAINTAIN THEIR TOOLS, DUCHENE!!!" I yelled.

Duchene lifted his head and very slowly opened his red droopy eyes.

He wagged his tail and yawned, then fell over on his side and clawed with his paw a little.

I took him out for a piss.

"Quit it!" I yelled, as he stopped and ate an acorn.

I opened his mouth with my fingers and traced his teethline and tossed out acorn fragments.

He licked his lips and finished a few small pieces, staring at me like fuck off.

I dragged the stick along the ground and ran up the rocky incline connecting the backyard to the driveway.

Duchene came sidewinding up, his ears bouncing all over.

We ran all over the yard and around the house.

"Good boy," I said, then pointed down and said, "Sit," and he sat by my feet, looking up with the white crescent eyes.

A tiny point of bone on the back of his head.

Big wrinkled cheeks and lips.

"You gotta lotta fuckin nerve, Duchene," I said, pointing my finger in his face.

He licked his lips and yawned, then pawed at me from a sitting position.

A truck with an enclosed bed came down the road and toward our house, at the dead end.

I grabbed Duchene's collar so he wouldn't run.

It was hard to make out who was driving.

Bunch of cages in the enclosed cab.

They did a three-point turn and left.

Amid the glaring brightness of the snow, I made out a face in the passenger's side.

A cold, distant-looking face.

"C'mon, Duchene," I said.

I tapped the stick on the ground off to his left, then when he looked I ran away to his right, dragging the stick along the ground.

He hopped up and came sidewinding.

Duchene was nimble and rugged, sure, yeah of course.

I poked the stick down between his front legs and he tumbled a little and got up, hopping around at me, his eyes wild.

I shuddered.

"Keep your fucking eyes open, Duchene, this world is gonna have its way with you. Being good-looking isn't nearly enough. You're as good as chum without me, Duchene."

He bit the stick and shook his head side to side, growling a pathetic, high-pitched growl.

I tugged on the stick and shook it side to side.

I ran him around through the woods a little.

He chased me but then fell in a pile of leaves and did an involuntary front flip.

Fucking Duchene.

I picked up a tennis ball and threw it; it bounced off the shed and went farther back into the woods.

Duchene didn't pursue it at all, instead lying down in the snow with a stick.

"Goddamnit, Duchene."

It was getting dark and hard to see.

I crept through the woods to find the ball.

"Goddamnit."

Branches poked my eyes.

I looked a little but couldn't find the ball.

Fuck it.

Then I heard something.

It was coming from the yard of the next house beyond the woods.

Sounded like whimpering.

I crept forward a little.

Saw a man carrying something into a cellar door.

The truck from before parked in the driveway!

A voice said, "You dropped one."

"Oh, I'm real sorry, boss."

As my vision sharpened, I saw the men come into the yard and approach something on the ground.

It was a puppy.

The men towered over it, looking down coldly.

The puppy looked barely weaned.

Just kind of wobbling there, wrinkly.

One of the men leaned down and lifted the puppy's ear.

He took a sniff and stood back up.

"This one is useless to me," he said. "Take care of it."

The other man said, "Yes, sir," and stomped down on the puppy, who was gone without protest.

I froze, my heart beating hard.

Fuck …

Tears formed in my eyes.

They began to freeze.

"Now listen here," said the main bad guy. "I'm tired of waiting, and I wish to move forward with the plan. I … must have him."

"Okay, boss, sure. What do we do."

"I've been studying their patterns. His owners are gone. It's someone else there. They get up around 4 a.m. every day. If we attack just before then, it should be easy."

"Okay, yeah."

"Every day, he becomes less of a puppy, taking with him my nn-nnngoodies. We strike tomorrow morning. In through the basement, take care of the sitter if we have to, snatch the goods and be gone."

"Sounds good, boss."

They crunched back through the snow.

I breathed out hard.

Yipes!

I ran back through the woods, tripping on sticks, snow falling on my head off of branches.

I ran across the yard, past Duchene, wagging his tail, and said, "C'mon stupid, let's go!"

I skidded to a stop in the slush and said, "Goddamnit," and fished an acorn out of his mouth.

"I told you not to fucking do that!"

He hacked.

I picked him up and ran inside.

[shot of just the dark backyard, voiceover]

"Duchene, get your act together, this is serious. We're being hunted..."

*

I paced the room as Duchene carefully tugged threads out of his rope toy.

"This is bad, Duchene, real bad. The Feds are gonna have my ass. We can't call the cops," I said. "They're gonna side with townies, especially if they come here, I don't live here, they find my gun or your coke, Duchene, our goose is cooked. Fucking charred. Plus what do I say, that I know a crime is going to happen? No. The cops are out. Hell, they might even be in on this … no, we have to, yet again, big surprise, do it ourselves. You in, Duchene?" I turned to look and he was destroying my boot. "Ey, STOP it."

I pointed my finger at him.

Then I got real close, pointing my finger right in his face.

"I'm up to my ass in brass, Duchene!"

I lifted his ear and took a big pull.

"Oooooooh," I said, reeling back and smiling with my eyes closed. "Just needed a little hit to get my mind going. Woo yeah." I refocused. "Okay. We gotta gear up, Duchene. It's time for war."

I wiped off my pistol and loaded the only ammo I still had, one ten-round magazine of some expensive "defensive" rounds, with bullets that looked like Phillips head screwdrivers, and extra powder in the casings, guaranteed to dump all energy at once, and fragment.

I put the magazine into the pistol.

Ten shots.

Ten shots to protect me and Duchene.

Ten shots to save the king.

The knight with only ten shots.

Be I.

I racked the slide back and let it slam closed.

The camera zoomed in on my face, smiling in a distant/ecstatic manner, and I quietly sang, "I'mmmmm dreaming, of a ... red Christmas."

And the Christmas lights my sister-in-law had arranged around the fireplace kicked on via timer.

And all was well within the manger of my heart.

Duchene wagged his tail a little, red-eyed and falling asleep on his blanket.

I put the pistol into a holster and clipped it to my belt on the small of my back.

If they wanted the goods, they could come for them.

I couldn't begrudge anyone a try.

But they couldn't stop me from stopping them either.

So fuckem.

"FUCKEM, DUCHENE!" I yelled.

It took him a full five seconds before he was actually awake.

He licked his droopy black lips and repositioned himself.

I quick-drew the pistol and held it out one-handed, staring one-eyed down the sights.

Duchene farted, and licked his lips a few times before returning to silent, deep breathing.

He was a good kid.

Really was.

*

I stayed up for as long as I could, but eventually fell asleep watching a romantic comedy, Duchene sprawled out next to me.

I awoke when, with fear in my heart, I heard the hum of voices in the backyard.

The scratch and crunch of footsteps.

It was just becoming light again.

I got up quickly.

Hid off to the side of the couch, gun in hand.

Duchene lifted his head and adjusted his bloodshot eyes.

Yes, stay there, bait.

Yes, I will protect you.

I'd left the back door purposely unlocked.

Come and get it.

I heard the suck of air, and the sliding of the door on its track.

Cold air.

My heart beat hard, arms jerking with sick energy, neck tense and biting down.

"All right hurry up," one said. "We gotta …"

Then he paused, breathing in sharply through his nose.

"Oh god, he's … beautiful."

I felt their steps coming toward me and Duchene.

So I rolled out from behind the couch, into a cool-looking crouch, pistol extended.

"Fuck you, creeps!" I yelled.

They paused, momentarily startled.

Duchene hopped on his back legs to play, breaching the muzzle, so I brought the gun down to the side.

"Goddamnit, Duchene!"

The men advanced.

One walked straight toward me, in what looked like a cloak with skulls on it, as the other henchman-like fellow chased after Duchene, who'd peeled off doing a sprint, thinking we were playing.

I tried to aim again, but the man in the cloak grabbed me, wrestled with my arms.

We fought for the pistol.

He squeezed my hand and it pressed down on the magazine release.

The magazine dropped and, as if sticking its tongue out at me, landed standing up.

The man and I wrestled, him holding my wrists, me pushing my shoulders into him to create space.

I purposely held the slide in place from the back, to not lose the chambered round.

This motherfucker was getting at least one pill.

Yessir, pappy had at least one vite-min for this fuckhead.

I remembered a move my brother showed me, where you pull them to the side one way, and then when they're off balance you pull them in and knee them in the face.

His nose popped.

He let go of the gun and backed off, groaning.

Trying to breathe, blinking.

I pointed the gun at him, one-handed.

Tried to aim but adrenaline said no.

BOP.

The blast rang my ears.

Room smelled like a burnt match in an oily garage.

The shot missed center mass, but hit his hip.

He immediately fell, clutching his side.

"Ugh," he said, blood coming out through his hands.

He crawled away directionlessly, pulling himself with his arms, blood smearing the floor beneath him.

The other guy had Duchene cornered behind the ottoman.

He grabbed Duchene by the scruff.

The man held him in classic hostage pose, knife to Duchene's beautiful face.

Fuck.

I was breathing heavy, holding the empty pistol, slide locked back.

"Put down the handsome good boy and nobody else gets hurt," I said, holding up my hands. "I mean it, creep!"

The guy holding Duchene yelled, "Don't fucking move. You move, I kill him. All we want is the fuckin ears, okay man? So don't … fuck around and this'll be just fine."

The cloaked man was groaning on the ground. "Help me, I'm … gonna bleed out," he said. "Please."

His henchman ignored him, tightening the grip on Duchene.

"Don't fucking move! You hear me? I'll kill him. I'll fuckin kill you. I'll kill fucking everybody!"

"Yeah, I bet," I said, narrowing my eyes and smirking. My smirk was very smug. "Only problem is, I know it, you know it, he's too cute to kill. You couldn't kill him if you tried, you fucking piece-of-shit creep."

The man swallowed hard, unblinking eyes on me.

He was a tool, and acted the part.

But had become self-aware.

He held Duchene around the neck, pressing a knife to his face, confident again.

"Yeah, and your only problem is, you're out of ammo," he said, nodding to my pistol. "Now step the fuck back." He walked along the wall. "And don't fucking move until we're out of here, or I kill him. I'll skin this fuck. I'm getting us out of here, boss, come over this way, come to me. Come on you can do it, let's go."

I stood there, watching.

Damnit, no …

Goddamnit, no goddamnit.

But there was nothing I could do.

The man holding Duchene slid the door open with his knee, stood there imploring his boss to crawl over.

I howled a little.

Duchene began to wiggle and squirm, his eyes wide.

Grunting and whimpering.

"Hold still, motherfucker," the man yelled, still eyeing me.

I howled again, much louder, accentuating the mournful sound at the end.

Duchene squeaked, his back arched.

"Stop it!" yelled the man holding him.

But Duchene didn't take orders from anyone.

He bit the man's face.

"Ah, fuck," yelled the man, dropping Duchene and holding his cheek. "That sort of hurt!"

There was my opening …

"It's been fun," I said, smiling, nostrils flared, "but I gotta roll."

I did a somersault, windmilling the pistol around and slamming it down onto the magazine, which was still upright on the floor.

Magazine in, I put my thumb on the slide release, smiled, and said, "Let it snow let it snow let it snow …"

Shik.

The song of oiled metal.

I raised the gun and fired.

BOP.

[ears ringing, eeeeeeeeee]

One hundred and eighty grains going a thousand feet per second, right into his shin.

Bone exploded out as he fell to a knee.

BOP BOP BOP, I put three more into his chest before he fell back against a table, sitting up, at which point I fired the remaining five rounds at his face, missing but once.

BOP BOP BOP BOP BOP.

Each shot flinging mist.

The slide locked back, chamber whispering smoke.

And when the ringing died down just a little, I found myself staring down the sights at a lifeless heap.

A lifeless heap in my sights.

I smiled.

"No evidence, Duchene. Fuck a jury. They'd skin our dicks for that ammo. They'd have our asses on a shish kabob, Cheney boy."

Blood covered the floor, tinseled by my sister-in-law's Christmas lights blinking on and off in the emerging dawn.

The lights went off then.

It was Christmas Day.

Another cold gray day in Michigan.

Lovely.

I sat on the ottoman, with blood coming toward my feet.

I set the pistol down, ears still ringing.

Duchene came skipping over and stood on his back legs, paws in my lap.

I picked him up by the armpits and he kicked his little back legs.

"Well, Duchene, we really did it this time."

He did a flip in my lap and pawed the air on his back.

I leaned down and lifted his ear, took a pull and smiled.

"You stupid asshole," I said.

The main bad guy made a groaning sound, having dragged himself over to the wall, where he'd propped himself up, holding his bleeding hip. "H-help," he said weakly.

I took my knife off my belt.

"Puh-please, no, please don't kill me," he said, with the puppy-skull shoulder-blade things scraping the wall as he backed up. "I'm sick, I can't help what I need. I can't help that I need it!"

"You know, sickos like you are all the same," I said, shaking my head and making a disgusted form with my lips. "It's a pity, really."

"Please, no …"

"What's that?" I said, pushing the knife behind my earlobe to make it look like I was straining to hear.

"Please …"

"Tell you what," I said, looking at my fingernails, "when you get to hell, tell Santa thanks, cuz I got what I wanted this year."

And then, by golly, I jackrolled him.

Just like the old man showed me.

Hitting him in the neck a couple times with the knife until it felt like I was punching a sponge.

The man choked like "glekk glekkkk," holding his throat, wide-eyed.

The last of his blood pissed upon him from within.

All over the floor.

I stood there breathing heavily.

Then I turned.

Duchene was sniffing the other dead guy.

"You gotta lotta nerve, Duchene!" I said.

And laughed.

Duchene walked over to his blanket, humped it a few times, did a few circles, and lay down in a quick heap, doing a combination of *oink* and *moo*.

Chin down and licking his lips.

His eyes were red and droopy.

He yawned a long slow yawn, his tongue curling out.

"Merry Christmas, bud," I said.

He sighed heavily as he settled in to sleep.

Fuckin Duchene.

Shh

Kathryn Scanlan

My surgeon's two big purebreeds, Buck and Geoff, led incredible lives. They ate top-shelf meat, delivered daily and ground by hand by the housekeeper. To simulate the stomach contents of small prey animals like rabbits and squirrels, the housekeeper included scant plant matter, some fruit. When my surgeon and his wife traveled, they picked resorts that catered to canine luxury: spa treatments, fine dining, elite sports.

My surgeon gave considerable sums—enough, by the sound of it, to support several sizable families—to animal rights groups. His wife was very particular about their leather. She rescued wrecked racehorses—doomed for glue—to keep as pets.

And when moles mangled his neighbor's matchless lawn, my surgeon slapped the neighbor on the back and said, *Live and let live, Al—what's so bad about a few lumps in the grass?*

But then my surgeon discovered an invasion of mice in the

climate-controlled garage where he kept his classic car collection. These were very special, very expensive cars, regularly loaned for films and magazines. The mice devoured the hoses of several engines. They soiled the seats and left dribbles and droppings along dashboards. In the glove box of his prized Porsche, a mother mouse birthed a litter of pups.

The exterminator recommended glue traps. I didn't think it through, my surgeon said. He shook his head sadly. The next morning he found them—cruelly stuck, alive, crying.

What did you do? I said. I was flat on my back below him, gowned and shaved.

Well, he said, I got my bag. I got my scalpel. I thought I could slice them off of there. They'd have clumps of glue on their feet, but they'd be free, he said.

Did it work? I said. Did you save them? A nurse fitted a mask on my face. Someone turned on the gas.

Well, no, he said. The first one I tried, I sliced off its foot instead. There was a lot of blood, actually. It was terrible, he said.

I opened my mouth, but only a little squeak came out.

Shh, said the surgeon. Over my face, his gloved hand hung— you could even say it twitched. Then, with two fingertips, he pushed the lids of my eyes shut. You've seen this move before—some man, overcome with shame, unable, for selfish reasons, to look at what he's done.

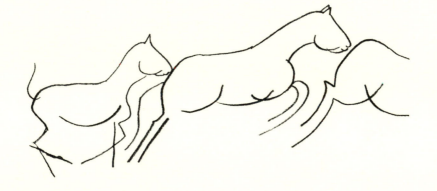

Training for Rio

Annie DeWitt

Paul pulled up in his golf cart and gave my legs a quick once-over. "Well," he said, "you look like you could ride." He was the type of trainer who believed half of talent was that a rider cut a decent figure.

We were standing ringside at HITS, a horse show facility in Saugerties, watching the $1 Million Grand Prix FEI CSI-5*. I hadn't seen a Prix since 1998. It was the end of August 2014. I wore a white straw fedora. Everything in the jump field was dry and sun-soaked. The dust from the footing cycloned under the horses' feet and clung to the inside of your nose. After every few rounds, large trucks of water went out into the ring and hosed the earth into submission.

Everyone went. Even the people from the town who knew nothing about horses. The Million was free. There was beer and enough lawn to spread out on. Who didn't want to watch a horse who cost more than your child's education fling itself over manmade objects so fragile one dip of a toe sent a rail crashing? The roar of the crowd echoing across the parking lot and back to the blue and white tented barns where the horses were stabled, waiting their turn at the circus? Modern-day gladiators in Hermes.

The thing you were looking for was *bascule*. Fifteen years out of the saddle I could still spot the fliers. The way a horse ascended and curved himself, catlike, over the rails. You don't want them to spend too much time in the air. Each second was precious. The good ones had hind ends that tucked up under them like springs. The bad ones got tight and jumped up head high, back straight as a board, like some ship on roller skates casting itself into the bay.

Show jumping wasn't my raison d'être; I was a wannabe eventer. Eventers are legendary for their versatility and grit. They ride in all three phrases—jumping, dressage, and cross-country. But I'd fled the city for a place upstate and was itching for the saddle again. I'd found a jumper barn that gave lessons and arranged to meet the trainer—Paul.

There's something postmodern about watching these animals who've graced battlefields and pulled tanks into war dressed in bell boots and bits and bridles of diamond-studded leather, small ear nets for the bugs tinkling in the wind. Made to jump around stadiums packed with corgis and labradoodles. A sea of polarized sunglasses so expansive that, from a distance, the crowd appears as one long windshield. A storm could wash over their eyes and they'd merely wipe the glass with their hankies and readjust the dogs on their laps. Each obstacle set in the ring was named after a bank or a watch or a car: Rolex, Land Rover, Longines, Wells Fargo. The brands printed on wooden wings flanking the brightly colored poles.

"Did he make it over the Marshall & Sterling oxer?" someone hisses to the body beside them on the bleacher.

"No. Dropped a leg and drifted in after the corner."

"What a shame."

The Olympics were the following summer and on everyone's mind. Paul was training for Rio. "I'm training for Rio," he said. "Normally I'd have a line of students around the corner but I can't take any of them on due to my training schedule. You, I'll give a chance if you're willing to commit to the program."

I met him at the barn the next week in an old white men's button-up I'd pulled out of my partner's closet. A riding helmet whose velveteen was slightly torn in the back. And a pair of chestnut Etienne Ainger boots I'd purchased off eBay one winter in the city. More fashion than function. I look back at that woman who walked into the barn and cringe. But if I didn't have the right gear, at least I possessed what every good rider needed: craft and delusion.

As with most things in life—sports, academics, love, real estate—when I got back in the saddle after a long absence I set my sight on unattainable goals with no plan for how to get there other than sheer will. It had been branded into me early: Go for the Gold. I'd always ridden two-bit horses—a flighty Morab purchased from the *Want Ad Digest* in 1991, a quarter horse named Star handed down to me from a trainer when the mare was too old and had navicular, my father's crazy Morgan Rebel who'd once pulled carts for some heart surgeon—but I'd always suited up for the job at hand. I washed my breeches, tucked my shirt in, and combed my hair back. I made do with secondhand Etienne Ainger.

Paul, I could tell, was of the same breed. A blond-haired, blue-eyed Argentinean who'd come to America on a nickel and a promise. The story of his upbringing was always changing. Some-times he had a brother who owned a coffee plantation back home; other times his wife was cleaning toilets just to buy him a pair of riding boots. It depended on the crowd he was in and the point he was trying to make.

Either way, the story went that Paul had started at the bottom. He'd arrived, he told me at my first lesson, at a fancy barn as a groom. He'd put his head down, shoveled manure, displayed his deftness with a currycomb, and hopped on any horse who would let him. One day a woman saw him ride and promptly demanded that he train all her horses. He was that good, or so the story went. The barn had swiftly elevated him to exercise rider.

What I respected about Paul was his understanding that class wasn't an inviolable set of circumstances but rather about attitude, talent, being a quick study. And, most of all, will. He was now head trainer at the private barn in New Paltz. A cozy Hudson Valley town a convenient two and a half hours north of the city, where enough money had commuted its way up the interstate to pack a whole Amish barn. The family who owned the property wintered their horses in Florida, and each year they flew Paul down to the Winter Equestrian Festival in Palm Beach to jump around with all the big names: Kent Farrington, Georgina Bloomberg, Eve Jobs. Once there, for a few thousand dollars, riders of all ages could take lessons with the riding world's Gordon Lish: a man, a myth, a leg-end who went by the moniker George Morris. Google "Jumping with George Morris" and YouTube will flood you with envy and glee. Paul claimed George as his mentor. Fashioned himself—in speech and style and practice—so closely after the guy that you might easily mistake the two in a dark alley. It was unclear whether they had ever met. Everyone in the jumper world claimed George Morris as their mentor, even if he'd only once glimpsed their horse across the ring and said, "Who's that hunk of meat?" This alone a glowing recommendation.

The afternoon after our first lesson, satisfied that I could indeed canter a horse around the ring, Paul took me in his golf cart up to the field behind the barn. It was there I met Joe, a skinny ex-racehorse, descendant of Secretariat. A pasture pet, all eyes and ribs, munching grass; no one had so much as put a saddle on him in half a decade. But I didn't know that then. What I saw was a great steed, a thoroughbred, who would once again rise to greatness under my thighs. It wasn't until later that Paul called him a "lawn ornament." "Has more jewelry in his fetlocks than the owner's grandmother left her in her will." "Jewelry," a tender term for the metal plates and brackets installed in racehorse's pasterns and fetlocks after they've run so long that things break down. Someone has to "pin fire" the cartilage around their cannon bones after the horse "pops a curb." Sew joints back together with steel plates. Horses' anatomy akin to two-ton tanks set on toothpicks.

"I'll let you have him for ten thousand," Paul said, looking at the horse's forlorn blaze. "All the eventers are riding thoroughbreds these days."

I didn't end up buying Joe, but I leased him. Picture me, the kid who grew up riding someone else's ex-pony, now riding an ex-racehorse at HITS on the Hudson. The gold flare of Margie Goldstein-Engle's boots a dim reflection in the brass of my freshly polished saddle tag. I purchased a Devoucoux jumping saddle from the daughter of the woman who owned the barn. The side of the green felted bag handstitched in gold leaf: Biarritz France.

Our second lesson, I told Paul a story from my days in Pony Club. I'd ridden Star one summer as a twelve-year-old in a tetrathlon—an event where you run, swim, shoot, and jump. My friend Sara and I had trained at the high school track and the Y. We carried gallon bottles of water roped around our arms to train ourselves steady. We'd taken the horses up to Vermont to compete. Despite my gangly awkwardness, I'd managed to be a proud third going into the final event: jumping. I'd suited up Star, headed into the ring, and jumped a clean round. My grandparents had driven down from Burlington. I could hear them next to my parents clapping in the crowd. But after the final jump, so flush was I with the energy of going clear, I'd hung a quick right around the standard and missed the finishing flags. I was swiftly eliminated.

The story had long crushed me. When I told it to Paul, his face set into stone. "That will never happen under my watch." As our lessons progressed, Paul invented increasingly difficult courses—some with fifteen jumps in a row, the pattern of which he'd change and I'd have to memorize on the fly, to improve my memory and spatial skills. Joe—bless him—was "more go than whoa" and never missed a pole. His energy built across the course so that by the end we'd gallop headlong over a cross-rail like a bullet out of a loaded spring barrel pointed at the fence on the ring's perimeter. That too Joe would have jumped, had I let him. I can still hear Paul's thick brogue from just outside the ring. "Pay attention, Annie. If you miss one stride, I'm sending you home." His were perfectionist tendencies. I beamed under the rigor.

Paul rode a white mare named Cara whom the owners of the barn had flown back from Argentina after Paul picked her out of a field on bloodline and confirmation alone. Her dam had been an

Olympian, Paul said. Her father a champion. Cara's one fault: she couldn't be kept on grass. She had an eating disorder, gorged herself on greens without filter. Twice a day she'd go in the "walker" where she was tied to a hook that circulated around a pole, like a merry-go-round. As the months passed and my knowledge of the sport grew, I realized that Paul was not in the class of riders "training for Rio." And that the jumper world was too plush with cash for my own taste. I wanted to get dirty. My dream: crashing through cross-country fences and natural obstacles on seventeen hands of pure-blood horse. How many times could you watch Jessica Springsteen jump around a $2 million animal with "Born to Run," her father's anthem, blasting over the tinny ringside speakers? Bruce often visible in the money tent where the only sound was the clink of Dom Pérignon and high-heeled Louboutins. This the anthem of America. I left the barn after a year to get back to eventing.

Over the next few years, I rode a six-year-old OTTB with the jockey name Never Naked in his first horse trials. Drove down to Virginia to work in a barn for an ex-Olympian in exchange for free lessons, room, and board. My parents and friends horrified that after a graduate degree, and a decade as a professor, I'd opted to get up at 6 a.m. in the muggy southern heat to feed, groom, tack, and shovel shit. The only difference between my mid-thirties self and that teenager training for tetrathlon with milk jugs on her arms was the fact that I'd packed my old Jeep with enough discount pinot grigio and whole wheat bread to get me through the summer.

Now I wake up at 8 a.m. each Wednesday to ride at a barn in Saratoga at the university where I teach before I go sling literature to warmhearted students. Their heads thick with dreams of doing what I do, which, in their mind, is "being a writer." On those days when the writing isn't coming and the world of words seems insurmountable, I hear Paul's voice in my mind. He's still riding Cara in the Adult Lows, one eye on the Grand Prix ring of his future. Dreaming of being the pinch hitter who gets the catch ride on the horse of a lifetime, takes that horse to the Olympics, and brings home gold. Often, when my partner asks me what I'm doing late at night still up on my computer typing, I boast softly in my best Argentinean baritone: "I'm training for Rio."

211

About the Contributors

RYŪNOSUKE AKUTAGAWA (1892–1927), born in Tokyo, Japan, was the author of more than 350 works of fiction and nonfiction, including *Rashōmon*, *The Spider's Thread*, *Hell Screen*, *Kappa*, and *In a Grove*.

ANN BEATTIE's eleven short story collections (most recently *The Accomplished Guest*) are filled with dogs.

RAEGAN BIRD is an artist currently living and working in Salem, Massachusetts. This is her first published story.

BLAKE BUTLER is the author of five book-length works of fiction, including *300,000,000*, *Sky Saw*, *There Is No Year*, *Scorch Atlas*, and *Ever*, as well as the nonfictional *Nothing: A Portrait of Insomnia*. His fourth novel, *Alice Knott*, will be published in 2019. He lives in Atlanta.

RYAN C. K. CHOI lives in Honolulu, Hawai'i, where he was born and raised.

MICHAEL W. CLUNE's most recent book is *Gamelife*. He is the Samuel B. and Virginia C. Knight Professor of Humanities at Case Western Reserve University.

PATTY YUMI COTTRELL is the author of *Sorry to Disrupt the Peace*. She lives in Florida.

ANNIE DEWITT is a novelist, short story writer, and essayist. Her debut novel, *White Nights in Split Town City*, made *The New York Times Book Review*'s short-list. Her story collection, *Closest Without Going Over*, which is in progress, was short-listed for the Mary McCarthy Prize.

CHELSEA HODSON is the author of the book of essays *Tonight I'm Someone Else* and the chapbook *Pity the Animal*.

YUKA IGARASHI is the editor in chief of Soft Skull Press, the series editor of PEN America's Best Debut Short Stories anthology, and the publisher of Fifty Storms, a showcase of new Japanese writing in translation. She founded *Catapult* magazine and was formerly managing editor of *Granta*.

KRISTEN ISKANDRIAN is the author of the novel MOTHEREST, as well as numerous short stories, which have been published in The Best American Short Stories, The O. Henry Prize Stories, McSweeney's Quarterly Concern, Zyzzyva, Ploughshares, Tin

House, and many other places. She lives in Birmingham, Alabama, where she is writing new books and working on opening Thank You Books, a new independent bookstore.

MARK LEIDNER's most recent book is the short story collection *Under the Sea*, called "virtuosic" by the *New York Times*. He is also the author of two books of poetry, *Beauty Was the Case That They Gave Me* and *The Angel in the Dream of Our Hangover*, and the films *Jammed* and *Empathy, Inc.*

TAO LIN is the author of *Trip*, *Taipei*, *Richard Yates*, *Eeeee Eee Eeee*, and other books. "Dudu (2007–)" is an excerpt from his forthcoming novel *Leave Society*. He edits *Muumuu House*.

SARAH MANGUSO is the author of seven books, including *300 Arguments*, *Ongoingness*, *The Guardians*, and *The Two Kinds of Decay*. She lives in Los Angeles.

SCOTT MCCLANAHAN is the author of *The Sarah Book*, *Crapalachia*, and *Hill William*. He is an economist and martial artist.

DAVID NUTT is the author of *The Great American Suction* (Tyrant Books). He lives in Ithaca, New York, with his wife and dog and two cats.

PRECIOUS OKOYOMON is a poet and artist living in Brooklyn.

SAM PINK brings the ham, you bring the mustard.

NICOLETTE POLEK is the author of *Imaginary Museums*, forthcoming in 2020. Her stories can be found in *New York Tyrant*, *Egress*, *Fanzine*, *Hobart*, *Chicago Quarterly Review*, and elsewhere.

KATHRYN SCANLAN is the author of *Aug 9—Fog* and *The Dominant Animal*, forthcoming in 2020. Her work has been published in *NOON*, *Fence*, *Granta*, and *Egress*. She lives in Los Angeles.

CHRISTINE SCHUTT is the author of three novels and three short story collections, most recently *Pure Hollywood*. A Pulitzer Prize and National Book Award finalist, she is the recipient of the New York Foundation of the Arts and Guggenheim Fellowships. Schutt lives and teaches in New York.

MALLORY WHITTEN lives with her partner, Chris, and their dog, Grace, in Ohio. She has published two books.

© Brett Castro

JORDAN CASTRO is the editor of *New York Tyrant* magazine and the author of two poetry books. His writing has appeared in *Tin House, Muumuu House, Juked, New World Writing, Hobart,* and other publications, and has been anthologized in four different countries. He is from Cleveland, Ohio.